No Small Comfort

Payton Himes

Kindle Direct Publishing

NO SMALL COMFORT Copyright © Payton Himes, 2021

The moral right of the author has been asserted.

All rights reserved.
No part of this publication may be reproduced, stored in a retrieval system, or transmitted, in any form or by any means, without the prior permission of the publisher, nor be otherwise circulated in any form of binding or cover other than that in which it is published and without a similar condition including this condition being imposed on the subsequent purchaser.

KDP, Charleston SC

ISBN: 9798505441831 (pbk)

This is a work of fiction. Names, characters, places, and incidents either are the product of the author's imagination or are used fictitiously, and any resemblance to actual persons, living or dead, businesses, companies, events, or locals is entirely coincidental.

To everyone who came back for more.

And for the boy who I doubt will ever read this:
Yes, he's based on you.

(If you have to ask: don't.)

Warning: This book contains descriptions of domestic violence and mentions of assault that may be upsetting to some readers.

No

Small

Comfort

1

Forty-eight hours after Wren went missing, the police showed up on my front porch.

I'd been waiting for them; they'd stayed in their vehicles flipping through paperwork and talking to each other in muted tones through their open windows, and so as they made their way up the steps, I already had the door open. I was ready – as I had been for nearly two days – steadying myself to hear them confirm what all of us had already accepted.

I told them what I never told her: that there had always been something about him that didn't sit right with me, that knowing this day might be coming didn't make it any easier to bear. I told them when I'd seen her last, and her condition when I had. I told them how she'd left, what she'd said, how she'd said it.

Sitting at a metal table in an off-white concrete room at the station, I answered the questions of sharp-voiced investigators about how I could tell the moment she walked through the door that something was different. How she said "I messed up," with such finality that I begged her not to go home.

Though they didn't ask for them, I didn't leave out the details of their past, or how many times I had interfered – both deliberately and unconsciously. I let them make their assumptions about me as I dragged his name through the mud. There was no point in understating the ire continuously burning beneath the surface. I even went so far as to clarify that I wasn't sure of the reason I disliked him so much; I wasn't sure if it was because I was just jealous, and how if that had been the case, I didn't want to know. This seemed to soften them, to humanize me, and to solidify my reliability. I loved her, and so I couldn't have hurt her. I loved her, and so I couldn't be lying.

But as far as they knew, so did he.

I didn't tell them how she stood on her tiptoes to press her lips to each of my temples, or how she rested her forehead against mine and stared at me like it was the last time she ever would. I didn't tell them about how she stopped my hands as I reached for her, to kiss my palms before she turned and left, her shoulders squared and her jaw clenched; because they didn't know her, and they didn't know that she never would have gone back if she'd thought it could end the way it did.

I didn't tell them that she looked like someone who was ready to fight, because the only way to make sure he never got another chance was to convince them that she knew she was going to die.

Over the course of the investigation and subsequent high-profile court case, details came out from all sides. The defense brought up her anger, her deception, and the precision with which she covered her own tracks. The prosecution annihilated them with a series of text messages and a single photo that I had taken while she slept on my couch one night: her hair falling over one eye, the other dark and swollen, her arm pinning a bag of frozen peas to the hollow beneath her ribcage.

I told them things I had promised her, on several occasions, that I would never tell anyone. I reassured myself that this would be what she wanted, if there were some way she could tell me.

But the biggest secret I kept came later.

Three years after I opened my front door to the police, I arrived home to a package with her name written on the return label.

Inside were letters: dozens of them, hundreds, all addressed to me and dating back to the weeks and months before her death. Letters in her looping handwriting, still smelling faintly of her lotion, telling me stories and raising more questions than they answered.

And so, for the first time in over three years, I sat down alone on my front porch, and I started to read.

2

The Great Love of My Life,

I don't really care which order you read this one in, because it's not supposed to be part of this and it's not numbered, obviously.

I'm at the post office, and they've just informed me that they can't mail all of these gradually over time several years in the future, at least not "with certainty that they'll all arrive" (which is concerning in and of itself, isn't it?!). Yes, I am aware that I probably should have done some research on that ahead of time. Planning is not one of my (many) skills.

So instead, they'll be arriving in one big box, which totally destroys the entire vibe I was going for, and also means that I take absolutely no responsibility for any lack of organization that may come with it. Complain to me in the future if you must.

I love you I love you I love you,
Wren

3

Dear Sawyer,

I hope this letter finds us well and far away from the address I've written on the envelope. If I'm in the room, do me a favor and wait until I'm not around to read any more – you know how much I hate watching people open gifts.

You told me to write you a story, and I will. But this isn't just any story; it's mine, and ours, and hopefully one that will be distant history and still in the making while you read it.

I thought the best way to celebrate ten years of friendship (and your 26th birthday, of course! The dates are close enough.) was with the very thing that started it all: a letter.

The plan is that these letters (yes! There are more to come!) will be far more extensive than the one that was folded up and passed to my desk a decade ago that simply read:

"I'll go if you'll go. – Sawyer".

By "going", you were referring to your (and, I suppose, also my) little town's idea of a good time: to cram as many teenagers as we could into the vehicles of the few who could drive, and make the 15-minute journey from Clearwell to Ochlockonee Bay. There, in the shade of knotted trees, blissfully ignorant (or possibly just careless) of the decidedly *not*-alligator-free waters, our tiny high school brought in the start of the new school year with hours of reckless, youthful shenanigans.

I splashed around ankle-deep on the bank a little; still

unsure about Clearwell as a whole and not yet convinced that it wasn't just some sort of unfunny, muggy joke. I was bitter and new to town and had never been good at making friends anyway. But I attempted, however weakly, and it seemed to be going okay.

Then the bonfires started, and the coolers cracked open to spill questionable beverages out to underage hands, and I suspected you knew the minute you passed me that note in Biology that this was definitely not my crowd.

So, it was there, somewhere slightly upriver from the bay, just close enough to make out the shadows shouting and cheering and splashing in the rapidly darkening blue-green water, that you and I became friends.

I was not an easy person to like, Sawyer. I was moody and quiet and I wore a lot of grey. You were (and still are) bronze and sandy and perpetually flashing your infuriating dimpled grin.

Maybe you just wanted a challenge. Maybe, even then, you felt the same way that I did in ways that we couldn't quite describe yet. Maybe you didn't think anything of it.

But I like to think you just knew.

Love, Wren

4

Sawyer Sawyer Sawyer,

We got very weird very fast.

Within two months of meeting you I knew what the school halls looked like upside down, and how your earlobes tasted. You would pause, raise one hand to your ear as though being spoken to through a wire, and we'd drop into crouches and scurry to hide behind the nearest object, barrel-rolling and army-crawling our way down staircases and around corners. I'd go home grinning, glowing, laughter bubbling over for the first time in years. Doug and Penny Ellis, for all their efforts, hadn't been able to have quite the breakthrough with their foster daughter that they had been hoping for. They loved you for what you brought out of me – they still do. You should visit them again soon; they always tell me how happy they are when you stop by.

Doug and Penny are the best thing that has ever happened to me after fifteen years of trouble and travel. My first night, they made my favorite dinner and told me that, if I let them, they would be my last stop. They would be home. They wouldn't force me to report what happened, they wouldn't make me talk about it; but they made it clear that if I wanted to, they were there. I repaid them by holing up in my room for the next three months, spending my first summer within miles of the sea tucked away in the dark. When I told them I was going to the Bay after several weeks of silence on the topic of school or friends or even acquaintances, they were ecstatic. They scrounged up fifteen dollars in case I wanted to bring snacks or buy dinner. Penny offered to let me look through her closet and told me she'd take me shopping that weekend. When you dropped me off at midnight, past curfew and waiting to make sure I got in alright, they were both still awake. They pretended that they hadn't been worried, but I could tell they had.

It felt good to feel loved.

On the way home from the Bay that first night, you kept the music low so I wouldn't have to speak too loudly to be heard, and you kept the silences brief and light. We'd left early, and alone, and you seemed acutely aware of the fact that, though we'd spent the entire evening together and my face was still composed and expressionless, I was perched on the edge of my seat as though ready to tuck-and-roll out onto the pavement at a moment's notice. What struck me the most was that you didn't mention it – didn't make light of it the way so many boys did, didn't point out my hesitation as though drawing attention to it would make it dissolve. Instead, you reacted to it, reflexively, quietly, keeping your distance and proving yourself to me in a way that was entirely unprovoked and earnest. Less than a day and one long conversation in and we were already beginning to read each other as though we'd been doing it for years.

I remember watching you drive off in your dad's car, still with all the caution of a newly licensed teenager who had nobody to impress, wondering what it was that made you pause until the front door was open and the light was trickling out over my damp and sandy feet. You know love, Sawyer. You've had it spilling over the edges of your heart your whole life. And so you waited those few extra minutes to make sure that girl you just met and didn't even know well enough to hug goodbye got into her house okay before you drove home.

I thought that was it, then. All those summer months spent reading articles and book fragments about the cycle of abuse, and I'd managed to avoid it.

That night, as I padded barefoot into my room and dropped my dirty clothing into a hamper instead of rolling it back inside of the duffle bag I kept under my bed, I realized I wasn't thinking about where I would go when this all went wrong, because it was like the warmth of you had seeped into everything else I had already been given and lit it from within.

I met you, and I loved you immediately, and for the first time in my life I genuinely thought that was it.

Love, Wren

5

Dearest Sawyer,

You invited me to your house under the guise of a belated 16th birthday party, though I still have my suspicions that it wasn't a birthday party after all and certainly wasn't for your own benefit (I admit that I may be naïve on the subject of birthdays, but what sixteen-year-old boy has a party several weeks after the fact, and demands that nobody bring presents?)

Your parents were thrilled to meet me, all smiles and praise and overwhelming kindness. Surprisingly (and yet not at all surprisingly, considering) you showed no evidence of embarrassment, just an almost invisible twitch of a smile tugging at the corners of your mouth. Apparently, you had told them all about me.

I was one of six guests, one of three girls. We sat cross-legged on the couches in your basement drinking Coke out of clear plastic cups and gorging ourselves on pizza off of greasy cardboard circles. We took turns playing video games, all of which I was terrible at (having never played any of them before), but nobody seemed to mind. CJ Turner, a girl from our Bio class who became my best friend (besides you, obviously, wipe that look off your face) until I drove her away in the same methodical fashion I did everyone else, told me stories about the town while she painted our toenails blood red with a bottle of polish she pulled out of her oversized purse. We played card games, knees touching as we sat in a ring on the carpeted floor, getting wholeheartedly and unironically excited about ridiculous little things. At one point, while bowing my head toward CJ's and strategizing in whispers, I made brief eye contact with you from across the group.

I don't know if you were aware of the look on your face, but I have thought about it every day since. You loved me, Sawyer. I've seen it a thousand times since and I've given it back myself, but here we were celebrating your birthday and you were more interested in making sure I was having fun. One corner of your mouth lifted just enough to shade in a dimple, your eyes soft and your head tilted. When our eyes met, you winked and the moment passed, but I carry the warmth from it with me even now.

I fell in love with the comfort and ease between us, how in sync we became and how quickly we did. I wanted people to see it, to notice it, to show me that it was not an illusion and that I really mattered to someone as much as they mattered to me. I wanted to catch them smiling at the casual way you handed me your Coke bottle after taking a sip, how you knew where my hand was even when you were too distracted to look for it.

We were already intwined at this point, had already latched on to each other in a way that was both juvenile and permanent.

I just love you,
Wren

6

Sawyer,

    It's a lot harder to write you letters than I thought it was going to be. Probably because I see you nearly every day. But you've always told me you wish you could see the world through my eyes, and so here it is:

    Our lives would have been so much easier if we had fallen in love with each other.

    We became something of a unit, SawyerandWren, the golden boy and his perpetually angry shadow. We must have spent half of our time in those first two years in your dad's garage – me reading on the corner of the workbench or cross-legged on a barstool while you worked tirelessly on vehicles I didn't even know the names of. I'd watch you through my lashes over the tops of my novels while you worked – and you never once acknowledged when you caught me. You were a sight to behold: lean muscles and broad shoulders and perpetual beach hair. You could have been spending your time with nearly anyone else in our world, and yet we chose each other. I had spent my entire life cast aside, whether by my own choice or others, and here we were; we had time for each other when we didn't even have any for ourselves. Even now, I'm writing this in the car while you work under the hood, though I could walk to the house from here and Cameron will be in one of his moods if I get there late.

    I don't think these letters will all be happy, Sawyer. But the world isn't all happy – especially through my eyes – and I know you'll prefer it this way. For now, I'm hiding each letter in the bottom drawer of the tool cabinet you've left just for me even though it makes all the other drawers a little bit crowded. I didn't even have to ask. You just made it mine.

See what I mean, about things being easier if we were in love?

I do love you, Sawyer. Probably more now than I did back when I told you every night before bed, whispering it into the phone as we both fell asleep. I love you more than I did when you came home early from vacation and surprised me at work, so that all the other ladies in the office 'awwww'd when I shrieked and jumped into your arms like it had been years instead of weeks. We've always had a flare for the dramatic, haven't we?

Absolutely,
Wren

7

Sawyer Sawyer Sawyer,

Right now, Shawn is in the corner, fiddling with that absolutely ancient black boombox that's missing half the dials and still has an actual, real-life antenna. I can't imagine that it is still working now (now being real-time, when you're reading this), although they do say things were made to last longer back then and it was clearly made before the dawn of time itself.

Don't get me wrong, I love all the Shop Guys, and I will always have a (slight) preference for you, but (and you can't tell any of them this, but especially him) Shawn is probably my favorite.

There's nothing wrong with the rest of them – Dustin makes me laugh daily and Ty was the one who decided to repurpose the old coffee can we keep in my drawer. Javier could double as a therapist and the few times Darren is around are always (delightfully) eventful.

But Shawn keeps hair ties on his wrist for me ever since he saw what a tangled mess became of the rubber band I used once in a pinch. He even picked a pack with what he dubbed "funky fresh colors" so that they would be easily spotted on the messy workbench. He has never chosen a coffee for me that was anything less than phenomenal despite me never branching out on my own. He once turned an absentminded doodle I drew into a full-page masterpiece using nothing but the stub of a #2 pencil.

We "went out" (if you can call it that – I think I speak for us both when I say we would have called it that at the time but wouldn't if we were asked now) almost twice, and when we realized halfway through our second coffee-and-walk outing that there was literally not the faintest glimmer of a romantic spark between us, we spent the next hour coming up with an elaborate handshake that we have continued to improve upon to this day. Three weeks later, when Javier heard about it and said, not entirely seriously, "if we'd known you were on the market, we would've made our moves sooner!" his eyeroll and bark of laughter was a perfect match for yours.

Before I came here, nothing came without conditions. But from the moment you brought me into the shop for the first time, with a sweeping gesture and a, "this is Wren", the energy in the room shifted to include me. I knew instantly from the looks they gave you that you hadn't actually needed to stop by, you'd just wanted to introduce me.

"I'm gonna be real honest with you, we thought you were an exaggeration," Dustin said as he wiped his hands on a rag and extended one out for me to shake, "not entirely fictitious, but definitely not entirely real either."

I laughed, and Shawn winked at me as he dropped the hood of the car he was working on and made his way over.

"Not that we're calling him a liar," he propped his elbows on the bench behind us and the two of you bumped knuckles, "just, you know, when someone raves about someone *so much*, you start to assume they can't really be as great as it seems. We stand corrected."

"Yeah, yeah, okay," you rolled your eyes, looping one arm around me in a loose chokehold to tug me closer, your laughter rumbling in my shoulders, "she already knows I'm infatuated with her, nothing you say can embarrass either of us."

"Also," I added, surprised and pleased with how steadily my voice came out even under the gaze of a room full of strangers, "he's basically my best friend, so I clearly don't feel embarrassment the way others do."

Javier, still elbow-deep in an SUV's engine compartment, threw his head back to let out one sharp laugh, and you rolled your eyes, grinning as you swung your arm around my shoulder and tugged me back toward you.

"Alright, clearly you're all a terrible influence on her, so we're gonna get going."

"Well, I'm sure we'll be seeing you again soon," Darren mused, perched above us on the countertop and wiping his mouth with the back of his hand as he ate his lunch, "after all, I think everyone needs a terrible influence or two in their life."

(The irony here is not lost on me; I think we can both agree I could have used more of that specific brand of influence).

And he was right, of course. Between you, Dustin, and Shawn I learned how to drive stick "well enough to save myself if I ever needed to steal a car". Over the years I've learned how to change a tire, how to change my oil, how to catch candy in my mouth from across the room and how to play card games that I'm fairly confident aren't recognized by anyone else on Earth. I spent afternoons here doing all the writing in your homework and mine (and sometimes some of theirs) while you all shouted answers to me from under or within your respective vehicles. I memorized takeout orders. I got mine memorized by them. And though by that point it shouldn't have surprised me, I still found myself regularly caught off guard by how the people you surround yourself with can become a genuine family of their own.

I have laughed harder within these four walls than I have anywhere or at any other time in my life – and with more frequency. I taught everyone how to braid (and let them use my hair for practice –

which did not always end well for me). We all gave each other completely unqualified life and relationship advice. I met girlfriends and siblings and even some parents (until I came here, my "parents" never wanted to meet any of my friend's parents. Given, I didn't really have any friends, but the ones that I did... someone really should have cared about who was supervising us).

Shawn just got the music to play again (a miracle, truly) and Ty looks like he's about to start dancing, so I should probably wrap it up and record him in the hopes of us getting fleeting but intense fame that we can reminisce on when you're reading this.

Famously yours,
Wren

8

Sawyer,

  All I know about either of my biological parents is that my mom was an addict in a way that did not allow for our coexistence to end in anything but disaster. I get why she made the decision she did once faced with a sudden reality (me) she wasn't prepared to deal with. It still sucks. But I get it. Angry though I was for so long, I can't say that I would have made a different choice, had I found myself in her position.

  I've considered DNA; I could send my spit to some website and see if she appears somewhere, but I don't know that she'd want to meet me even if I found her – and I don't know that I'd want to meet her, either. Not because I bear her any ill will; on the contrary, I owe the person I am and the life I have here to her decision to let me go, though it couldn't have been easy for her. But because I have a hard time meeting new people, and she would be new to me, really.

  Every once in awhile I think about it. I wonder if she would see the resemblance between me and the tiny, sickly infant she handed off to a nurse at an urgent care. Maybe she gestured to the signs in the window that said "no questions asked", maybe she didn't even wait to make sure I was in someone else's hands before she left – I don't know that I'd be able to blame her for that, either.

  And then there's the fact that I have no way of knowing how much of the story I've been told is true. I'm so many degrees removed from anyone who would know for sure. No matter how many times I change my mind, if I commit to anything then that is as far as my control goes; once I've made a decision then everything that follows is out of my hands entirely.

I really am trying to make this not all about the train wreck side of my life, which means I need to talk more about you. But we're both kind of full of ourselves, so I'm sure you'll like it.

I backed out of everything close to a dozen times when we first met, and you never once got mad.

First, I wouldn't hang out with you alone (the night of the Bay didn't count – even in the shadows there were other people slipping past, voices echoing). Then I wouldn't come to your house. Then, once I would, I wouldn't stay once it started to get dark and it became easier for words to spill out.

As dusk settled over us one evening, I unfolded myself from your couch and reached for my phone.

"If you stay, Sparrow, I promise I won't kiss you."

The things that come out of your mouth, Sawyer.

"Okay?" and the things that come out of mine, awkward and stilted and unrehearsed.

"So stay," you smiled that infuriating one-dimpled grin, holding out your hands, palms up, "that's what you're leaving for, right? Well, I won't."

"Should I be offended?" I rested my knee on the cushion, half-lowering myself back into my spot, "because I feel like I should be offended."

"I didn't say that I find you repulsive. I just said I won't kiss you. I didn't even say 'ever', although that can be arranged."

I could feel the corners of my mouth fighting my resolve to keep a straight face, and I extended my hand out toward you.

"Swear."

"I pinky swear," you reached out, hooked your littlest finger through mine, "that I will never kiss you on the mouth unless you explicitly ask me to, which, given the face you're making, seems unlikely. Should *I* be offended?"

"Probably. You're gross," I told you, and you laughed and my heart fluttered like it always did when I did anything that earned your approval.

Maybe these things stick in your head the same way that they do in mine, but the weight of them is comforting. Two weeks later, when hurricane-speed winds kept you from driving me back home, you lent me a pair of your sweatpants and a t-shirt that fell loose off my shoulders and over my hips. We stood side by side at the bathroom sink, brushing our teeth and crinkling our noses at each other's dim reflections. We all slept on inflatable mattresses on your basement floor, though you and I spent most of the night in your room a few feet away, watching the rain pour down in sheets on the other side of the glass and picking winners in raindrop races while your parents snored softly on the other side of the door.

"Are you crying? Are you okay?" you turned toward me, your hand cupping my chin in the wind-speckled shadows. Something about the dark and the quiet and the effortless tumble of our personalities drew a nod out of me and then the words.

"Yes. And yes."

"Why?"

"Is it weird if I'm really happy right now, and that's why?"

You grinned, just slightly, your perfect teeth and your one divot of a dimple flashing.

"Yeah, but you're weird, so it's alright."

We stared at each other for a moment, lightening shimmering across us and sending the shadows dancing, and then I tilted forward and pressed my lips to your cheek.

When I sat back on my heels, my heart and stomach rose in my throat as the entirety of us hung in the balance, because we fell into place fast, Sawyer, but that only meant all of our falterings and missteps happened quickly and efficiently, not that they didn't happen at all. But you smiled, softly, gently, and the warmth of you spilled into my veins.

"Alright, Sparrow."

Alright,
    Wren

7

The Great Love of My Life,

For one summer, we were normal.

We hung out in groups, in packs, in gaggles of long-limbed girls and boys with newly broadened shoulders.

CJ and I were inseparable, all bowed heads and curtains of hair as we whispered to each other. I'd catch your eye from across the room or the fire or the table, and she and I would dissolve into giggles that would make your jaw shift like it does when you're trying not to smile.

She taught me how to French braid, and bargain my way to deals at flea markets, and an assortment of moves from the various self-defense courses she had taken.

Of course, you remember this, because though you and I still gravitated toward each other as though we were tethered, there were also a lot more question marks in our texts to each other, specifically from you.

Can we hang out or are you busy?

What did CJ say before you left today?

Did you know your nose crinkles even when you're laughing at other people's jokes?

Before, everything was staccato – rapid-fire letters zipping across town to light up each other's faces.

Home.

Noon?

Here.

I see you!

Our actual conversations were spun with our temples touching and our pinkies linked, but that is not the story for this letter.

You like her too, don't you? She's fiery and loud and oftentimes everything I wasn't. I loved it right away. She made us all laugh so hard that tears streamed down our cheeks and our stomachs ached.

I asked her, once, and only once – because we had more important things to talk about than boys, even you – if she would date you. On one of the sizzling nights that summer, when she and I lay the long way across her bed, blankets kicked off into puddles beneath our bare feet, stripped down to camis and cutoff shorts.

"I've never seen him look at me the way he looks at you," she said, in that jokey disbelieving way she used so often.

"Sawyer doesn't look at anyone the way he looks at me," I said, still laughing, and this set her off again.

That's what she whispered to me, that night we left your house.

Look how he looks at you.

She and I got a job together at the animal shelter where her aunt worked; we walked dogs and cleaned litter boxes and stuck vegetables through the bars to scarlet-eyed bunnies. On weekends, we'd take her car to the mall and I'd sit, cross-legged and straight-spined, while she tried on sundresses and canvas shorts and impractical heels, the two of us doubled over with laughter as she tottered across the fitting room floor.

"Please try this on," she'd beg as she held up vibrant flashes of fabric, strappy sandals, thin-strapped sheaths. Sometimes, when my stubbornness outlasted hers, she'd buy them for me; her face lit up in unadulterated joy as she presented them to me in the parking lot.

It was worth it, of course, when my stinginess paid off and I was able to afford my very own car at the end of the summer with only a little help from Doug and Penny. It was dinged up and rattled and squealed in protest on rainy mornings, but it was mine.

But it was worth more than that – those countless trips zipping down the freeway to get to the mall with all the good stores, music blaring, windows down. These were nothing like the yellowed tile floors of the shopping trips in my youth, no used tennis shoes already molded to someone else's foot purchased from a secondhand bin on a dingy carpeted floor. These shops were brightly lit and pulsing with pop-music remixes, mirrors with edges angled to show you infinite copies of your shimmering frame, and associates who handed you little blue mesh bags instead of eyeing you warily from behind the counter.

Here, there was no squeezing your feet into sneakers an inch too small so that nobody would know you've grown. No cutting the tags out of your jeans because they chafe your skin – but really because they put a number on how much your hips have widened since you were 13, a measurement of your self-loathing. She taught me how to undo my long-practiced transformation into someone a half-size smaller than I was.

"Me too," she'd muse at the faces I pulled in the mirror, tossing me another pair of shorts while I shimmied out of the first pair, "I swear these mirrors are made to make us hate ourselves, but that's life."

And it was a transformation, to acknowledge myself. To recognize and yet be more than a size, a number, a measurement. To have clothes that fit right and a laugh that echoed down halls and friends who didn't shift uncomfortably whenever I mentioned my past.

"You know, you can always tell me this stuff," she said once, over smoothies, our shoulders tilted toward each other at the tiny table we shared, "and I won't ever judge you. The past happened, Wren. You have to let it out."

In the documents passed on to the Ellis's along with me was a brief and slightly inaccurate description of why I was being transferred from one home to another. I say slightly because, while it did touch on the frequency of sexual abuse in the foster care system, it came nowhere near close to describing what my foster brother had done to me. It was easier that way – writing it off as an incident – because without a report, without my consent to give a report – there was no case, no mess. I was sent away as a temporary fix to a problem that would just rear back up for the next poor girl.

I had always found it ironic that the Safe Haven law was what got me into what had been a fairly hellish existence, but once I found Clearwell and the family that came with it, I guess it sort of made sense to me.

I told her about my previous foster family before I even told you. She had stories of her own, and yet she wasn't broken.

"Everyone has something," she'd tell me, when the truth got too heavy for either of us and we'd sit silent, staring out the windshield for a few moments too long, "some people just can't bear to talk about theirs."

We drifted, once things started to change. Cam didn't like the way she brought out the fire in me, the resistance – he didn't like the way she stared too long at him without giving an inch except for the gentle twitch of her eyebrow. I let her slip away much easier than I did you. And yet she was still a vibrant smile on the streets and a warm hug catching me off guard in the baking aisle. She was still an alibi who lied through her teeth for me without ever asking me why. There was something about the secrets we had shared over all those iced coffees and late nights that made her understand how I would respond to continued pressure, and so she let herself be edged out with the grace of someone who would never say 'I told you so' if and when I finally let her back in.

    She's good.

Your wing woman,
Wren

10

Sawyer Moore,

We've spent a lot of time wandering around places we probably shouldn't have been. I discovered Geocaching and you threw yourself into it with a passion and enthusiasm I had never seen before. Thank you for doing that. The excitement, I mean – I know the treasure hunts were also for your own benefit.

We'd explore abandoned buildings and duck into dark, cramped rock hollows. On multiple occasions we found ourselves unsure of where we had come from or how to get back the way we came, instead seeking out roads and walking in whatever direction seemed the most promising. It was on these journeys, the heat and humidity curling the hair around my ears and making the skin on your hairline glisten, that our comfortable silences were solidified. Most of the time we were alone, and then I was fine; matching your pace by taking a step and a half for each of yours, taking your hand to help myself onto and around places you traversed easily. I let my knees get dark and my hands smudge dirt along the highs of my cheekbones as I wiped away sweat, and I never thought twice about it.

But occasionally – especially in the first few weeks of summer, or just after our return to school, when your presence drew in people I would have never imagined myself spending time with otherwise – occasionally we went in groups. Our silences, our choppy and intense discussions, our ease; all of them were suddenly cut into by complaints or questions, my footfalls redirected to make space for others. Bitterly, I wanted you to make them feel unwelcome, but never in all the time I've known you has that been something that you've been capable of.

And so I made time for you when they couldn't – not for you but for myself – staking a claim in a person who wasn't mine in spite of how it may have seemed.

Around this time, you started paying a lot of attention to people (specifically, girls) who were distinctly not me. I didn't have a problem with it – at least not outwardly; please don't feel guilty for my shortcomings (though I know you will).

And yet, unfairly, I was angry and jealous of the girls whose teeth were perfect, whose stomachs were toned and whose clothes always fit perfectly, who drew your attention that was usually reserved for me. I caught myself rolling my eyes when they'd laugh at your jokes, or when they'd sweep their hair over their shoulders in response to your proximity.

There was no way for me justify my bitterness to you without sounding jealous in all the wrong ways. Once, when I mentioned offhand (and uncalled for) that your most recent flirtation had a bit of a mean streak, you flashed me one of your dimpled grins and said simply, "you know I've only got eyes for you, Sparrow."

It's not your fault, and it wasn't theirs, either. Every reason I gave for disliking them, which I felt were mostly justified, was tainted by my own confusion.

But they were long-limbed and slender-waisted and demanded your attention in all the ways I wouldn't, and so when they followed along on our adventures I found myself shifting in my own skin, faltering in ways uncomfortable to me and foreign to you.

It's still not your fault. I know as you're reading this that you're replaying it in your head, moments where your hand grabbed theirs instead of mine, when you leaned into them subconsciously and didn't even notice the toxicity of our glances in each other's direction.

But it was always me that changed. I adapted, I accepted, rather than forcing the world to do any of it for me. I recognized my misguided indignation, and I overcorrected.

When you see into my head, does it make sense to you? When you – even unintentionally, with only the purest of intentions – found yourself drifting, I altered myself. When he did the same, so did I. But his intentions have never been pure, Sawyer. I see that now. I know. If you're reading this, something has changed. Or maybe I've just stopped.

Love, Wren

11

Sawyer,

Remember when we were sixteen and the AC at your house broke? Our entire world was 102 degrees and humid, and you refused to put on a shirt or pants or anything but your boxers, despite me insisting with increasing levels of frustration that it was your duty as my friend to suffer with me.

"If you do not put on a shirt right now, I am going to take off mine," I warned you, and you rolled your eyes like you didn't believe a single word coming out of my mouth.

Honestly, I hadn't either, but you know I could never step down from a challenge, especially an illogical one.

When your mom got home and came downstairs to tell us she'd brought home ice cream, she found us both sitting on the couch in our underwear: me reading, you playing videogames, and it still remains the only time I have ever heard your mom yell.

You at least had the decency to look sheepish, dragging a shirt over your head and leaping into your shorts, but I was secretly ecstatic at the prospect of somebody caring enough about me to get mad when I made irrational decisions, and so I kept my back to both of you, biting my lip to keep from grinning too widely and giving myself away.

"Do not ever let me catch you two doing anything like that again," she warned, and I think we both knew that she wasn't exactly sure how to approach the situation, because we nodded and didn't argue or explain ourselves at all, "I don't even know what was going on. But it wasn't appropriate, and I feel like I should scold you for it. So I am. There's still ice cream, but I'm going to eat it first and I expect both of you to sit here and think about how ridiculous you are for a few minutes."

Even when dealing with us, your mom managed to keep a level head – impressive, because if I ever have kids anything like the two of us, I'm sure I'll lose my mind far before their teenage years.

I had grown accustomed to the parents of my friends treating me like I was going to contaminate their children – watching me warily from across the room regardless of how polite I was or how wide and unassuming I made my eyes. I think your mom sensed that from the start, and so your parents never faltered, never so much as flickered in a way that would suggest I was anything less than who I was. At first it felt like pressure; I walked delicately, afraid that any lapse would only prove to them that their confidence in me was misplaced. But their expectations of me fell level with yours, and I grew into myself before their eyes.

That night in August, when you found your mom and I sitting on the porch, she tethered me down.

She drew the conversation from me without me even realizing it was happening; one minute she was making tea for both of us and the next she was asking me if I was going to stay.

"It's not really up to me," I said, not entirely bitterly but not entirely cheerfully, either, "I haven't really stayed in one place all that long before."

"Do you want to?"

I was afraid to nod, afraid to admit that this was the first place I'd been where I didn't feel like I had to live out of my backpack. She took a slow sip, staring out across your lawn, giving me a moment to respond and then speaking when she could tell I wasn't going to.

"They love you, you know. Doug and Penny."

I still didn't say a word, my eyes flicking toward her and then back into the bottom of my cup, knees pulled up to my chest and elbows tucked against my sides.

"I think Sawyer would really miss you, if you left," she mused, shooting me a sidelong smile and drumming her fingers gently along the edge of her mug, "and we would, too."

"I'd miss it here," I said, so quietly that she let it slip past, only nodding slightly and not making eye contact.

"Don't be upset with him – he was only answering a question I asked – but Sawyer told me about what happened with the other family. The one that was going to adopt you."

I didn't find any anger inside of me for you, only a hum of curiosity, of energy.

"Doug and Penny aren't going anywhere, sweetheart," she turned just slightly toward me, her knees almost touching mine on the porch swing, her voice soft, "they've been settled here for a long time and I think they plan on being settled here for even longer. And they want you. Nothing would make them walk away. Do you understand that?"

The earnest gentleness in her voice, in her eyes, made me nod, just once, hesitantly.

"Now, they won't bring anything up with you that they think will scare you, or make you worry. And if you don't want them to adopt you, that's alright. But Wren, honey, they love you, and if you let them, they will keep loving you all their lives."

I found myself silent, wide-eyed with disbelief and something like awe, biting my lip to keep it from trembling.

You stepped out onto the front porch and plopped down between us on the swing, stretching your arms along the back so that the moonlight spilled blue and vibrant across your chest. I wove one ankle around yours like a habit, and you gave my shoulder a gentle and absentminded squeeze.

I stared out across the lawn and the stars sparkling in the puddles on the street, critters buzzing and singing in the trees, and for the first time in my entire life I knew I was home.

Love, Wren

12

Sawyer,

  Shortly after we met, your parents decided to treat me as though I was their own.

  Dawn and Terry Moore have been one of the best gifts I never would have thought to ask for. Maybe I was the daughter they never had. Maybe I brought out the same spark in you that you brought out in me. Maybe it was just my ever-dazzling personality and sheer power of will that made them love me.

  I was always welcome to come over for dinner, or lunch, or breakfast when we had whole days planned. I got to tag along on family vacations, and somehow it was never embarrassing when your mom gave me the hand-me-downs of her friend's daughters – it made me feel loved, and permanent, and connected.

  We went to New York for six days in August, spending our time alternating between overbearing humidity and sudden downpours that ended just as abruptly as they began. Your parents ordered a cot for the hotel room we all shared and insisted that you sleep in it instead of me. We sat in the bathroom with a towel shoved up against the door to stop the light from spilling out, playing card games and telling stories.

  "Everyone thinks we're dating," you said, like you were announcing the weather, or what color my shirt was.

  "Unsurprising," I responded, earning a smirk, and that was that. Never again did we discuss the possibility, or the rumors. We didn't need to. We knew.

In what must have been an attempt by your parents for us to experience all extremes known to man, we went to Minnesota in the dead of winter, and spent a week in Duluth in a lakeside hotel despite the fact that it never got above 5 degrees. Every morning, while your parents still slept, we would silently put on what seemed to be every article of clothing we owned (and yet somehow still not enough) and hobble out across the creaking snow to watch the sunrise. It hurt to breathe, our lungs dusting frost onto our eyelashes, and we paced to keep from freezing in place; mornings spent hopping on planks of ice thicker and clearer than windowpanes, before shuffling back into the hotel dining room for coffee that burned the whole way down. They would be awake by the time we slipped back into the room, planning the day and welcoming us both into the warmth of their blankets like we were six years old.

In the two and a half years that you and I knew each other before Cam and I started dating, we went on vacations to places that I had never even dreamed I'd get to go. We slept in the back seat of your parent's sedan while they drove into the nights, leaning until my head rested on your lap and your body slumped over mine like a cocoon, exit streetlights flitting over our skin. You woke me up, wordlessly save for a whisper of my name, to watch neon lights cast a glow over red rock and shadowed parking lots at 2am. We dragged duffle bags and suitcases into motel rooms just outside of major cities, still sticky with sleep from the car ride. There are pictures of the two of us with our arms flung out triumphantly at the Grand Canyon, Rockefeller Center, the Golden Gate Bridge.

"We're going to California," you told me, and when I didn't react with quite as much enthusiasm as you thought was appropriate, you leaned in closer, "Wren, *we're* going to California."

I began tagging along with your family immediately, so effortlessly on my own part that it wasn't until our third vacation that I realized I may be overstepping my bounds.

"Don't be ridiculous," your mom told me, but she said it so kindly that it didn't make me feel small at all, "we're going anyway. We wouldn't have nearly as much fun without you."

We always took detours to find people willing to show us their self-sufficient homes, where they lived almost entirely off the grid. You'd pull up coordinates on your phone and yell "TINY HOUSE!" and your parents would, rolling their eyes and trying not to smile at our excitement, turn the car in whatever direction we needed to go. You even took a class on them your first (and only) full year of college, sending me pictures of your textbook with unadulterated enthusiasm. But really, why would you need a huge house when you could live in such a cute little one? Your parents always humored us, except when it came to all of the cheesy tourist attractions that your dad refused to drive to on principle.

I spent so much time at your house with you that I started "helping" you with your chores, and they started giving me a weekly allowance just like yours. Sometimes, when they weren't around and I spent more time throwing popcorn at you than helping, I guiltily gave you half of mine. I know you snuck it back into my bag. It's all in the bottom drawer of your dresser with all the extra blankets, wrapped in the old red pillowcase.

You're welcome,
Wren

13

The Below Average Love of My Life,

Whenever I was stressed, you'd come home to find me lying flat on your bed with my arms outstretched, my gaze falling somewhere between my face and the ceiling. You'd settle along my side, silently, resting your face against the space beneath my ribs and flinging your arm across my abdomen, the other stretching out above your head to link your fingers through mine. There was (is) something extremely comforting, grounding, about the weight of you, your breath rising and falling until my heart rate had lowered and my eyes would close. Your parents would wake us for dinner gently, unearthing us from heavy and contented naps that left us bleary-eyed and unsteady on our feet.

You called me Sparrow, because wrens are birds and sparrows are birds and I was flighty. You'd trace the hollows on the insides of my arms, the spaces between my fingers, point out the delicate joints and angles. I felt softer, lighter, made up of feathers and fluff in spite of my sharp edges.

But, as nicknames do, it would become something else entirely if spoken too loudly, and so it stayed between us. In front of our friends, you called me Tweety, or Robin, or Chickadee. They stuck fast, all of them, but Sparrow was and still is ours.

In what I'm sure was an obnoxiously short amount of time but felt like ages after we'd met, we started trying to one-up each other at every opportunity. I'd introduce you as my father; you'd introduce me as your aunt. When servers commented on how cute we were together, I'd gasp and insist that you were my brother. You were my cousin, my therapist, my husband. Once, when running into an elementary school teacher of yours, you swooped me close and said, triumphantly, "this is Wren, the Great Love of My Life."

And so it was, catching eye rolls and snorts from everyone who knew us, knowing and disbelieving smiles from our elders and peers. When it was getting late and Doug and Penny thought it was about time for you to be headed out, they'd play along, knocking on my bedroom doorway and suggesting that my One True Love should be on his way home soon.

"Close, but I'm Great," you'd say charmingly to them while you head-butted me gently in farewell, sashaying down the stairs and out the door like a breeze.

At the many diners we swept through on our vacations, you'd kick me under the table and tell the waitress I was The Great Love of Your Life, and I'd tell her, wide-eyed and somberly, that I hated you.

"Sawyer," I'd say, and her eyes would follow mine to the dazzling smirk on your face, "I'll start a new life right here in this town without you."

"Oh yeah?" you'd retort, and she'd look back and forth between us like she was watching a particularly aggressive tennis match, mouth slightly ajar, "well I'd start a new life right here in this town *with* you."

Deal.

Love, Wren

14

Dearest Sawyer,

The first time I called your smile infuriating, you smiled harder.

You've got a trustworthy mouth, you know that? Your crooked little smirk, your impressive set of dimples, the way you carry yourself like you know exactly what effect your smug grin has on people. Your mouth looks like it would be good at keeping secrets; and it is.

It's always been infuriating, how good-looking you are. You're the kind of gorgeous that gets tacked up on the bedroom walls of teenage girls and kissed goodnight. I hate it, and I hate you for being so damn attractive that I want to keep you all to myself despite the fact that I'm not (really) attracted to you at all. I wish we were in love. I really do.

Girls can be so nice to each other, you know? We'll fall all over ourselves gushing about how good that dress looks and how great her makeup is and how incredible we smell. Guys don't do that. But they really should. It would do all of you well. It's good to hear nice things about yourself for no real reason.

I remember one night, probably six months after we met. We were watching TV in your living room; you were ridiculously sprawled out on the couch and my head rested on your stomach as it usually did, even then.

"You smell like sunscreen. And ink," I told you, splaying

your fingers out and pressing my palm to yours so that you'd fold your fingers over mine, then bringing them close so I could inhale the warmth of your skin, "and motor oil."

You buried your face in my hair, and I felt strangely self-conscious for the first time since I'd met you. Then you exhaled and settled back in.

"You smell like citrus. And vanilla. And something... distinctly Wren," you replied, and then your face was suddenly very close to mine and I feared for a split second that you were going to kiss me. But you just grinned, and I pressed my thumbprint against your right dimple, cupping your chin with my other four fingers.

"Your smile is infuriatingly charming," I said, and when you smirked, I added, "you're pretty infuriating overall."

"Charmingly infuriating," you agreed.

I have always been someone who fears change even if it's for the better. I used to make you promise that you were not, nor would you ever be, in love with me. And yet we both hoped, didn't we? Because it would have made sense, had it happened. We have always had something just short of platonic.

Love you much,
Wren

15

Sunshine,

    I never realized how much easier it would be to write everything instead of speaking it. And that's really saying something, considering the unending stream of consciousness that I have been verbalizing since nearly the moment I met you.

    But here, I can tell you about how sitting down to dinner with Penny and Doug started off as something that felt more formal to me than it did to them, and turned into something I looked forward to every evening.

    A lot of the places where I lived gathered up all the kids for dinner every night. Sometimes it felt like an interrogation, others it felt like a genuine attempt at stability. Still others felt like an obligation, like they had to have at least one time per day where they could see everyone in their care and confirm that we were all alive and accounted for, and dinner was the most convenient for them. It also allowed them to make sure that we were all eating, since most of those places kept the food locked up to avoid us hoarding it in our rooms or eating entire family sized boxes of cookies in the dark pantry in the middle of the night.

    So I didn't exactly know what I was getting into, with Doug and Penny. He cooked, and she set the table, and then we all sat down with our hands folded in our laps and smiled kind but stiff smiles at each other for several uncomfortable moments before lifting our forks. I ate small bites, slowly, pretending not to notice as their eyes flicked back and forth between me and each other, until finally Doug cleared his throat softly.

"Taste okay?" he asked, gesturing to my plate, his voice a half-step too high and his face rearranged into an expression I recognized as *deliberately non-confrontational*.

"Great," I responded, cringing inwardly at the way my pitch rose to match his, and then set my fork down and cleared my throat too, "it's just I... have trouble eating in front of people. Sometimes. Sorry."

There was the briefest pause, one where they both blinked and I waited for someone to scoff or gesture aggressively for me to leave the table. But instead, Doug reached past Penny to the corner table where he'd left the mail beside his keys and wallet, and placed the newspaper on the table beside him. After shuffling through some pages and selecting one for himself, he handed it to Penny, who did the same. I felt my brow furrow slightly as I watched them, as she passed the remaining bundle to me and snuck a sideway smile at her husband.

"Mind if we sit here with you while we read?" he asked, and when I shook my head, he held my gaze for a moment before dropping it to the page before him and reaching once more for his fork.

"We don't mind distractions at the dinner table," Penny said, smoothing her own paper down at the edges, "it's sometimes nice to just be near each other for a bit at the end of the day."

It didn't take long before the newspaper stopped being read, and even less time after that before it stopped making it to the table at all. And then I was in the kitchen chopping vegetables and stirring sauces, and when I talked with my mouth full nobody took away my plate or sent me out of the room. We would text each other while they were at work and I was at school, planning meals and sharing links to recipes. There was a sudden, unpredicted normalcy about food and eating, about likes and dislikes and being able to leave the yams virtually untouched on my plate if I didn't want them.

And once we crossed that hurdle, the entire world opened up in front of me. Forgive me if that sounds dramatic – I do have a flair for it, after all – but you don't realize how much food and eating impacts the rest of your life until you realize you're not thinking about it anymore. I could go out with you and CJ after school and not just stick to coffee, or eat the pizza the guys ordered in to the garage without worrying about seeming greedy or ungrateful. I could socialize with my peers for the first time for as long as I could remember – because socialization is so often about food, isn't it? – and focus on them instead of what I was putting into my body.

Then came the dinners – all six of us around your parent's dinner table or mine, a clatter of dishes and clinking of cutlery and a never-ending stream of conversation. Us on the edge of the porch while Penny and your mom swayed on the swing and the dads did their dad thing at the grill, clicking tongs and inspecting burgers. Picking up takeout on those days when it suddenly felt like we'd been apart too long and didn't want to waste a moment.

I was so lucky, so suddenly. I don't like to think I took a second of it for granted – because in retrospect, even the mundane moments were a glimmering delight.

Brushing chip crumbs off this page,
Wren

16

Sawyer,

    I'm going to tell you about when it was good, so that maybe you can understand why I've stayed when it's not.

    You know some of it, obviously. But before this. Before it got bigger than just me.

    I told you, in bits and pieces, about our first date. It was my first date ever, as you'll recall (and I'm sure you do, because you teased me mercilessly and with the kind of exactness that can only come from already knowing exactly how I would respond).

    You weren't exactly his biggest fan, him being roughly eleven years our senior while we were still nearly a year away from graduating. But he charmed both of our families, keeping a respectable distance until they'd warmed up to him. It helped that he was nearing the end of his residency – being well on his way to being a pediatric surgeon made him seem softer, less dangerous.

    Of course, at the beginning, he never seemed dangerous at all.

    You said it once, and only once: "what does a 28-year-old want with a 17-year-old, Wren?" and when I insisted that we were only friends (which we were, then) and that he didn't want anything (a lie, obviously – but I didn't realize it at the time), I must have seemed offended enough that you didn't bring it up again, at least not so directly.

    He had come back to live near home, and only a short

commute to the nearest hospital. We met when some of our friends and some of his coworkers went to the same Denny's in the middle of the night – them because they'd just come off a shift, us because we were 17 and thought we were cooler than we were (though, to be fair, we were pretty cool).

You and I were shooting other people's straw wrappers at each other from opposite ends of the table when he came over. A momentary hush spread over our group, like we were expecting this guy to tell us off for being too rowdy. But instead, he set a napkin down on the table in front of me, his number and *Cameron Stone* scrawled across it legibly but messily, and smiled.

He's got a killer smile when he wants to.

"I'm sorry for being so forward," he said, quietly, stooping so that it was clear that though he was audible to the rest of you, he was only speaking to me, "I just couldn't let the opportunity go by."

When he walked away, our friends whooped and hollered, and you shook your head and rolled your eyes, but you were trying so hard not to smile and gave yourself away. I ducked my head, feeling my cheeks go crimson, and stuffed the napkin into my jacket pocket. I didn't text him for over a week, and when I did I immediately threw my phone halfway across the room in fear.

I've wondered, since, what he saw in me that called to him.

I've tried to remember the distance between me and the nearest person at the table, tried to recreate my body language to see if something about the way I was sitting revealed that I was not part of this world but had rather fallen into it. Did I seem so easy to lead away, to topple, to twist? Or did it start off as something genuine? Did he ever really have that in him?

But he was friendly, and cautious, and made a point of keeping his distance and acknowledging the age gap right from the start. Even you found it difficult to find fault in him, though you tried harder than everyone else combined. Time passed. "Chance" run-ins at the mall turned in to long conversations which turned into texts which turned into him showing up when we had friends over. Everyone wore down.

And so, the night of our first date, the night the ground first started truly shifting beneath me, I brought an entire duffle bag of clothes to your house, changed in your bedroom, and modeled them for you while you waited on the couch in the living room. You pretended to be disinterested, but shook your head and wrinkled your nose or shrugged in faint approval nonetheless.

You sat cross-legged on the edge of the bathroom counter while I painstakingly applied my makeup, retouched my hair, and rethought my outfit a dozen more times. When I faltered, you grabbed my face with your hands – careful to keep from smudging my hour of hard work – looked me in the eyes, and told me that he would be a fool to be anything but amazed at the sight of me.

You also told me that you'd have your phone on you all night, that our code word was "retro" (as in that "little retro diner" we went to on special occasions), and that you'd come get me in a heartbeat no matter what time I needed you.

He took me to a restaurant that didn't make me feel underdressed. I ordered salad and lemonade – glaringly obvious in my attempts to stay inexpensive – and he gently insisted I try the steak.

By the time our dinner arrived, I had relaxed considerably, and he had rolled up the sleeves of his button-down shirt and leaned back in his chair. We talked about his job and my plans after graduation (which didn't involve college, due to the whole 'foster kid has no money' situation). We talked about lighthearted things like our friends and our hobbies and places we wanted to see.

He was fairly well-traveled, having gone on frequent road trips and vacations with his parents in his childhood (this was before he told me that his mom had left them years before, and before he told me why), and that stirred up something in me that I hadn't realized was even there. I wanted to see the world. I wanted to live day-to-day, wandering without worrying about plans or money or my future. I wanted to see things I had never been given the opportunity to see, and know that I had somewhere to come back to.

We shared a slice of key-lime pie for dessert, and I consciously paced myself so as to not eat even close to my share.

He drove me home at 10:30 sharp, and we sat, unbuckled, in his sleek silver BMW for close to half an hour, tying up the loose ends of conversations and lingering on the still-uncertain success of the night while the butterflies in my stomach fluttered violently and I wondered whether I was going to throw up or faint.

"You're just as fascinating as I thought you'd be, Wren," he said, softly, and my heart swooped and my hands shook so hard I clenched them in my lap to hide it. I didn't know what to say, so I didn't say anything at all.

He didn't seem to mind my silence, smiling and leaning in to press a gentle kiss to my cheek. I still don't know whether he would have gone in for another (though I suspect he would have, had I hesitated), because in my nervousness and general awkwardness I fumbled with the door handle and ducked out backward, nearly tripping over my own feet.

"You text me first this time," I said, my voice surprisingly strong for how weak I felt, and one corner of his mouth went up in that cocky little smirk that I grew to love (and then to hate).

"Goodnight, Wren," he watched as I sidestepped onto the lawn. I didn't wait to see if he was still watching, but was acutely aware of my every move as I made my way up the yard and onto the front porch.

He was gone by the time I reached the front door.

Here we go,
Wren

17

Sawyer,

On our second date, Cam and I got ice cream and walked on the beach. It was breezy, and the sun was golden on our skin, and I remember wishing there were a graceful way to walk through the sand that didn't involve swaying my hips like I was balancing on a tightrope. We sat with our toes in the waves for awhile, nibbling on our cones and showing off tiny shells that had washed up around us.

Every time we made eye contact the butterflies in my stomach would kick into motion again and my cheeks would flush, and he didn't pretend not to notice like you did.

"I like it," he said, smiling when I ducked my head, "it's almost like seeing what you're thinking."

When we stood to walk back to his car, I tried to brush the sand off the backs of my legs as inconspicuously as possible, and he winked at me and averted his gaze.

There weren't any red flags, at first. There weren't any warning signs in the moment. They're easy to see, now, jutting out of the space between his fingers when he reached out to pull my face toward his, cutting off my nervous rambling and setting a precedent for future interruptions. They're waving violently overhead when he innocently inquires about my relationship with the guys in the shop and then does a poor job concealing the suspicious downturn of his mouth. They're whipping and flapping in the background when he slides my phone out of reach, silencing a call from Penny and insisting that I can call her later while pressing kisses to my neck.

Here we are later, me giving up when his anger reduces to a simmer and he's pinning me into the corner with his hands on my waist. There we are walking through the mall and me keeping my eyes trained on him so that he doesn't suspect me of looking at anyone else. This is my new normal, with him insisting that they haven't called, and I should be able to do this on my own now, because they aren't my real parents anyway.

Little by little, piece by piece.

But I didn't feel any fear in the pit of my stomach when he reached out and spun me, the dim solar lights lining the boardwalk flickering beneath our feet, grinning when I laughed and twirling me around and around until I leaned into him dizzily. I wasn't scared when he took my hand and pulled me along, the two of us running with our shoes dangling from our fingertips and sand spraying out behind us, the waves hissing on the shore and the distant hum of cars singing back. I was only nervous when we rode the Ferris wheel skyward because his pinky was linked with mine and the stars twinkled in his eyes.

Everything was magical, because as long as I wasn't looking, there was nothing to see.

Maybe there still isn't,
Wren

18

Sawyer Sawyer Sawyer,

On our third date, Cam and I went out for coffee.

We sat across from each other at a table so small that his knees perpetually brushed against mine. He ordered us those fancy little coffees with the pictures in the foam, and laughed when I got some on my upper lip. We played Dots and Tic Tac Toe on too many napkins.

"I really didn't realize how young you were," he said, tilting his head and flashing that tiny little smirk, "I wouldn't have guessed if you hadn't told me."

"Nobody ever thinks that about me," I took a small sip, ducking my head, because it was (and still is) true – I'm always mistaken for a teenager, a preteen, a not-old-enough.

"You're an old soul. It's the eyes."

"The things I've seen," I joked, and his face softened, fingertips grazing mine.

"Where has life taken you, Wren?"

We stayed until the place closed and then we walked along under the streetlights. Somewhere along the way his hand found its way to mine. My skin lit up where his thumb traced figure eights.

He didn't ask me much about my childhood because he didn't want to talk about his. At the time, I assumed it was because he knew I wouldn't want to talk about mine.

He did talk about work, a lot. About his coworkers and

about their escapades and about the various emergencies and tender moments he had been privy to all the way since the start of his residency. I realized after hours that I had hardly spoken once, my chin resting on my upturned palm and my eyes wide with fascination. Somehow, it still felt like a conversation despite it being almost entirely one-sided. He had a way of making you feel like you were part of his story even if you weren't.

He made me feel special in a way I never had. He'd chosen me, out of everyone and anyone else he could have. I was different. He told me so.

We sat on a park bench in the thick evening air, angled toward each other, his arm outstretched along the back so that his fingers grazed my shoulder every so often. And I focused so much on the slightness of his fingertips and the crook of his mouth that I didn't think to look for anything else.

Love, Wren

19

Love of my Life,

I'm not sure where I got my name.

You know this, because we talked about it in the blanket fort we made later the same night that we became permanent, the winds howling against your house and your parents sleeping in the next room.

It never bothered me, the not knowing.

We laid there for hours, staring at the same point on the ceiling, shadows falling over us even heavier than before, temples touching. I remember things differently. You've told me that. They're more vivid, more focused, deeper than your own memories of the same moments.

"If you could pick your own name, would you pick the same one?"

"I already can pick my own name. Who's going to stop me?"

You laughed at that, still occasionally surprised by the quickness of my retorts.

"Is that a yes?"

"I don't know. Sparrow's good, I think. But it's probably even harder to find that name on a mug."

It was a prologue to future conversations, and who we'd be if we could change everything ourselves.

Because of my Safe Haven origin story, I don't know who

named me. I don't know if my mother left it pinned to a notecard on my blanket, or if she even left a blanket at all. I don't know if it was the nurse that realized she wasn't coming back for me, or the first foster mother I had. I only know that I was sick, and small, and furious at the world even as a newborn. Could I trace myself back to the very beginning, if I tried? Maybe. Probably. But we've been over this before.

Maybe I got my name in the same way I got the one you gave me. I have no doubt that I was flighty and narrow and delicate more so then than I am even now. Maybe the nurses that stood guard over me in the hospital traced the fragile angles of my bones and smiled at the ferocity of my squalling and named me for it. Maybe they hoped it would help me fly.

"Would you want to know?" you asked, as though you had read my mind, had followed the path my thoughts had taken, "or is it better to decide for yourself?"

"This way," I stretched, arching my back and letting my fingers graze yours as if by accident, "this way, it is whatever I want it to be. It's better not to know, for me. I know enough."

"Sparrow," you mused, stretching yourself, but this time you hooked your fingers through mine and didn't pretend you didn't mean to, "the baby who named herself."

When I laughed, you turned your head so that our eyes met, and you shimmered all the way through me.

Love love love,
Wren

20

Mr. Me,

In a little wooden box in the bottom drawer of my dresser in my parents' house, I still have every note we passed to each in school.

There are tiny little stick-figure drawings of the two of us scaling the margins, bubble-lettered teenage woes hardening slowly into neat lines of plans and jokes and storytelling. We dated them, in the same way we dated all of our papers, with tidy numbers printed in the upper right-hand corner.

Unlike me, you have always been good with words, but, like me, you've always been better with them when you're given time to use them how you want. It's for this reason that our best conversations happen when it's just the two of us – because there is no discomfort in our silences, no need to fill emptiness with sounds.

It's also why I've kept your notes; the words, even when still stilted and youthfully unaware, often strike hard and fast and resonate even as we age.

Some are nonsensical out of context, jokes and quotes that were hilarious in the moment having faded with time into something that only makes the corners of your mouth twitch with vague familiarity. There are things you think you'll remember forever just because they're important now, and then one day you realize that everything else has taken priority in your mind. And so quotes become confusing, and stories change minutely with each retelling, and eventually some things stop being told at all.

We'd get creative with folding, practicing elaborate tucks and twists and pleats to make eavesdropping on our scribbled conversations an impossible feat. It always seemed to come naturally to you, but I can admit now that I spent many nights in the blue light of my laptop screen, creasing and un-creasing dozens of sheets of paper, running my thumbnail across the edges to make them crisp, hoping that I would remember my way through them the next day without the diagram in front of me. It wasn't necessarily to impress you – though I'm sure at the beginning that played a larger role – it was just that things always seemed to come so much easier to everyone else, and I wanted to maintain that illusion myself.

None of them were ever put back together quite right anyway, so in the end, it was just another way to show off.

We never got caught, and I still maintain that we owe that entirely to the fact that we were good (for the most part) kids, and so our teachers probably paid less attention to us than they should have. We grew a little too confident, but that will happen when nobody tells you 'no'.

I reread them sometimes, and find myself sprawled out on the bed in a sea of college-ruled paper worn soft around the edges from years of being handled. I sort them by year, by class, by mood, try to remember what it was we were going through that made our words so angst-ridden.

My favorite, bent at so many angles it has hardly any space left for words, in your tight and angled handwriting says,

"We'll title this in our minds: things we'll never do, and why."

Of course, I have absolutely no idea what we were referencing, or why we never planned to do it, so I have no way of knowing whether we were telling the truth or not. But it still seems accurate. How many times do we see other people making the same mistakes as we are, and still we pretend we're different? It's easier to pretend. We do it every day.

You started addressing your notes to me with a tiny drawing of a bird – not a wren, probably, but we didn't care enough to be accurate. I started signing them with the same bird. Eventually, it disintegrated into a simplistic arched line, like the silhouette of the lone member of a flock flying overhead. And then, still later, it turned into just a 'v'. And suddenly, there was another nickname, I was someone else entirely for a moment. Anyone who would have intercepted our notes (but who would? We were hardly interesting) would have seen you speaking to someone who didn't exist. Those are the best kinds of nicknames – the ones that start from happy circumstance and become something on their own.

Anyway, I've hidden notes in every nook and cranny of your car, so I hope you haven't sold it by the time you're reading this.

Love, Wren

21

Sawyer,

Here's the thing: I'm not in love with you.

But I love how you can tell, on early summer evenings and late fall afternoons, that I am not all alright. You know that I am all too familiar with when the sun is filtering white-gold through the trees and speckling your bare skin, and the air is just cool enough to make the tip of your nose tingle, and something deep inside of you has come undone.

I love that you make me feel all angles and narrowness, your sweatshirts coming down halfway to my knees and falling over my hands. You make everything between us effortless, and you make things with other people simpler.

I love that I can find your eyes across the room and speak to you without saying a word, that you've never made me feel unwanted for the sake of a joke. I love that you are so genuinely eager to teach me new things, to make learning them as effective and exciting for me as it is for you.

I love that you hear the bad things that come out of my mouth so easily in front of you, and you take them in stride. When we were sixteen and rowdy, you discovered the bruises following the segments of my spine and questioned them. I could tell you were expecting a different origin, but when I confessed that I had never had such constant and unrestricted access to food, that I found the places in my room where the floorboards didn't creak so that I could burn the calories without alerting the rest of the house, you didn't try to stop me. You just nodded and your eyes followed mine until you felt confident that I'd talk to you again.

I love that Doug and Penny talk to you, that they love you, that their faces light up when they see us together. I love that they know that you are where my secrets are safe. I love that they trust you with them, despite knowing how dangerous they must be.

I love that you make me laugh so hard I stop being self-conscious about it. You make me stop being self-conscious about everything – even things that I can't get out of my head with anyone else.

Here's the thing, Sawyer. I'm not in love with you. But I love everything about you, and somehow, that includes myself.

Love me love you,
Wren

22.

My Dearest Sawyer,

You just saw me writing this, and, when I wouldn't let you see what it was, you told me I should write you a story. Little do you know.

After I finished writing yesterday, and locked it away in my drawer, I swiped your credit card and went to get us lunch. We drove down to the river and ate on the hood of your car, sharing fries and drinks. I'm only telling you this because you have a terrible memory and by the time you read this a little over three years will have passed.

When we finished eating, you called your dad and got the afternoon off. You had a shimmer in your eye that I haven't seen in a long time. You always get that look when you're doing something you shouldn't – even if you have permission.

I had a sudden vivid flashback of the two of us crouched under the staircase by the cafeteria doors, three days after that evening at the Bay. I'd snuck out of my last class of the day right after attendance, and you hadn't gone at all. Whenever I'm in the crisp silence of a tile-floored hallway, I think of us hidden there, holding our breath, waiting for the footsteps of a passing teacher to fade. I turned my head so my nose almost brushed the spot above your ear and whispered, "if Penny finds out I skipped class, she'll kill me."

I felt you smile, and you grabbed my hand and lead me out the doors and to your car like you'd never been scared a day in your life. You said, "she doesn't have to know."

And she didn't, until a year later when I confessed it to her when she'd suggested that she and I skip a day together, just to get it out of our system. She wasn't mad – I think she felt she couldn't be, given the circumstances and how much time had passed – but I noted her sidelong glance at me and the way she pursed her lips nonetheless. I always smiled when they scolded us.

But yesterday, there was nobody to tell us no. We had the entire day to ourselves, and we spent it in the shade of the trees down by the Bay with the sun speckling our skin through the branches. We didn't talk about him, or anyone, really, just ourselves and the things we've done and plan to do.

We're going to really hike in the Grand Canyon, and mountains, and all of the worst roadside attractions we can. Maybe, by the time you're reading this, we already will have. I like to hope so.

Because here's the thing, Sawyer: I have a ritual for every time I see you.

After you drop me off, or I walk home, I take off every article of clothing I wore near you and throw them into the machine with his. I add too much detergent and fabric softener. I wash them twice.

I take a shower so hot it burns me, and I wash first with his soap and then with mine. I make sure to scrub raw the places that touched you – my shoulders, my elbows, my hands. I hold my fingers to my face while the water runs angrily over me, and I inhale until I don't detect a single iota of you, of oil, of sunshine. I change into something he likes – either one of his shirts or something unassuming – and I dry our clothes.

While they dry, I clean. I line up our shoes. I make sure there's no dirt on the soles of mine that could give me away. I sweep, dust, distract myself with making sure there is no evidence of your continued presence in my life. I act, for all intents and purposes, like someone who is having an affair. I try not to think too much about it.

After our clothes are folded, hung, and put away, I settle in with a book or my laptop and wait for him to come home. I can usually tell before he even walks in the door whether it's going to be a good day. Funny – I used to relax at the sound of your footsteps coming up your front porch, and I feel every muscle in my body coil tight at the sound of his. I close my eyes and listen to the way his key turns in the lock; if I'm lucky, and he's in a good mood, he won't be upset with me for not letting him in.

Whenever Cam has been away for longer than usual – on Thursday nights or when he's out of town – he's suspicious. He always has been. I remember thinking once that it was sweet that he cared. Now I hold my breath when he hugs me because I know he's inhaling so deeply as he pulls me in to see if he can smell you on me. I think sometimes he gets angry even when he can't.

He asks me about my day. He waits for me to trip up. Sometimes I do, and he snaps. Sometimes I don't, and he does anyway. Other times, when I'm preparing for the worst, he's soft; when I lower my eyes and try to get him to talk about himself, he presses his lips to the top of my head and ghosts his fingers along my spine, gentle and achingly kind.

He has always loved to keep me on my toes.

Delicately,
Wren

23

Sawyer,

Two years ago today, you picked me up from a police station 5 minutes from Alabama.

That one sure was fun to explain our way out of.

I never thanked you enough for being so calm. It's not every night you get a phone call begging you to drive 2 and a half hours to bail your frantic friend out of jail for trying to take stolen property over state borders.

When they brought me out to meet you, you smiled even though we both knew there was nothing funny about the situation.

"You her boyfriend?" the officer asked as he handed me over, clearly too tired and too old to want to deal with either of us.

"Nah. He's the one who left her here," you looped your arm around my shoulders with such ease that his question didn't surprise me at all.

"Ah, well. He's not pressing charges. So you're good to go. You stay out of trouble."

The two of us didn't say a word to each other until you'd pulled onto the side of the road just outside of town.

"I'm sorry."

"I would have given you a car," you said, so bluntly that I lost my words for a moment, "if you'd asked, I would have given you a car and he would have had nothing substantial to get you for. Hell, Wren, I'd drive you out of here myself."

"Then let's go," I leaned over the console, made you look into my bloodshot eyes, "right now, Sawyer."

You called my bluff, like I knew you would. Instead, you gestured to my split lip, the way I kept my arm tucked to my side like a broken wing.

"What'd the cops say to you about that?"

The taste of blood had already grown familiar to me now, my tongue running over the raw corner of my mouth.

"He said he'd hit me, too, if I usually act like this."

You laughed, but it was sharp, humorless. Your hands gripped the wheel like you were wringing a neck.

"I just spent six hours in a concrete room because my boyfriend is mad that I tried to run away," I told you, "I am twenty-one years old, and I still get grounded."

You used to grab me by the back of my neck and rough me up while you planted big dramatic kisses on the top of my head. You'd jump on me, grab me from behind, throw me over your shoulder and bite the place where my stomach met my ribs. You used to make me shriek, and you'd laugh because I always did, too. I used to sprint up behind you and jump onto your back with no warning; something inside me always felt warm and weirdly loved from the way you'd hook your arms under my legs to catch me almost instinctively, without breaking from your conversation. I'd bury my face in the crook of your neck and breathe deep, inhaling the smell of your skin like a drug because it felt like home to me. If you didn't pay me enough attention, I'd nibble on your collarbone until you'd drop me, and I'd settle into the space under your arm like I was made to fit there.

Don't you see how it made sense for him to be jealous? Don't you see how I had to stop touching you, loving you, seeing you?

You aren't rough with me anymore, and I don't blame you. I am fragile and I crumple even before impact. You move slowly, deliberately, so that I know where each word will land before you've even spoken it. Today when I got to the shop and saw your legs jutting out from underneath the car you're working on, I had a vivid image of you sprawled out on my bedroom floor, tossing a ping-pong ball up and catching it, occasionally pausing to bounce it off the side of my head when you felt ignored. That doesn't happen anymore, and not just because you're not allowed in our house.

But that night, while I told you about my cellmates and tried to ignore the fact that Cameron might actually kill me if he saw you drop me off, you were so gentle. Your fingers wove through mine and your thumb traced circles on the back of my hand.

You told me that you loved me enough to do it, and that's why I couldn't. Your family is too golden, and you are too good. When I go, I will go alone, because I cannot bear to take you with me.

You are so good,
Wren

24

Sawyer Moore,

Remember that place we used to go, just slightly too far of a hike upriver?

The sun streamed golden through the trees and dappled our skin, the breeze off the water captured the shadows and cooled us to the touch. We'd lie elbow-to-elbow, glass bottles wedged into the sand between us, letting the sky bronze our skin and paint my cheekbones pink. Eyes closed, chins angled upward, we'd spend entire days hidden away.

I'd go alone, now and then. Sometimes, the walk seemed longer than ever, and I'd wonder if we'd imagined it – or if it only existed when we were together.

But then it would appear before me, nestled into the rocks and roots, and I'd settle down with my book and read until there was just enough sunlight left to get home by.

I've always been sad, Sawyer. Quietly sad. It hums in my bones constantly, heating me up from the inside out. It's always there, even when I can't hear it, but the longer I find myself in silence, the louder it grows until the air is heavy with it and it drags me down by my knees. It's something you learn to live with.

But you understood. I'd turn to face you, my head lolling on the lukewarm sand, and hold my hands up so that sun ghosted through my fingers, low and bronze.

"Yeah," you said, when my lips parted and then came back

together without a sound.

You are white noise at the worst of times and a symphony for the rest of it. You drown out the murmur and lift the weight.

The last time we went, the ground was littered with cigarette butts and the burnt remnants of cheap beer cans, and I saw the look on your face and knew you understood, too.

Something changed, and it wasn't just because someone else had been there. It was because someone else had been there who didn't care.

We've found other places. And we've made enough noise to smother the darkness. And the whole time, you've understood.

Love, Wren

25

Sawyer,

      I'll tell you the truth, for once, but I'll spare you the details.

      You knew, the morning after, though you pretended you believed my excuses. You knew as you pulled up alongside me and reached across to push the passenger door open, as I ducked in and slammed it shut on us, tucking my legs up against me. You didn't say anything for a few minutes, and then, when you did, the slight shake in your otherwise calm voice told me why.

      "I thought you were waiting. Taking things slow with him."

      "I am."

      "That's not what it looks like."

      "Well, it's not like you'd know."

      The look you gave me was humiliating. The mixture of disbelief and hurt that flashed across your features was almost enough to make me apologize, but, considering everything that was rushing through my head, I didn't.

      "I'm not covering for you. Not for this," you said, though we both knew you would if I needed you to.

      "They're not going to ask, Sawyer. Nobody's going to ask."

      "So, what? They think you were at my house last night?"

      "Probably, I don't know."

      "Really? You're going to lie to me, Wren? To me?"

      I turned on you, my mouth quivering, my arms still crossed tight over my chest.

"I'm not lying to you. I was on my way to your house last night, and he picked me up. Sorry I didn't tell you. I didn't realize that you and I had to make official plans, now. We hung out. Nothing happened. Can you drop it?"

Your jaw tensed and your hands tightened on the wheel, but you didn't speak. I could see the gears turning in your head, your teeth grinding.

"Sawyer," I said, my voice breaking, "I just really need you to not be mad at me right now."

You weren't. And somehow that was worse.

"Are you okay?" you asked, after a pause just long enough to get under both of our skins, and I didn't answer.

But you did drop it, and you didn't mention it again for a long, long time. If you had, maybe I would have told you. Maybe I would have explained to you that I *was* waiting, that I *didn't* want to. That I *had* said no, again and again and again, but that eventually I had stopped. That I still felt dirty and ugly and wrong under my skin from what had happened to me years ago, and that Cam had assured me, promised me, that this would be different.

It wasn't, Sawyer. It was exactly the same.

It took awhile for you to stop looking at me like I'd hurt you on purpose.

I know, now, that it wasn't that you were angry with me. You could feel it already, the poison seeping into us. You were mad, yes – but you were also scared. Scared for me before I was even scared for myself.

A few months later, when he first brought up the idea of me moving in, he couldn't understand why I said no. He never understood why I said no. He never tolerated it, either. Just over a year after the first time he hit me, I was living under his roof.

I thought that was just how it was. How it was going to be. You made sacrifices for the people you loved, the people who loved you. But nobody ever told me that you're not supposed to sacrifice yourself.

You were livid when you found out how quickly, how easily I'd give in if it meant he'd stop being so angry, so forceful. You used words like "conditioning" and "manipulative" and "rape". It was the last one that got me. I shoved you, tears burning in my eyes, my voice catching in my throat.

"Don't you dare say that to me. Don't you dare make this into something so ugly."

"But it is ugly, Wren. What he's doing to you is disgusting."

And I always had the same excuse, the same denial, the same reasons. *He loves me, and I love him, and that's what you do when you love someone.*

Only a few times did you ever try to make the unforgiving comparison between the two of you. The *I love you too, Wren, and I would never.*

"That's different," I'd say, every time, "it's different love."

"Well I'd sure as hell hope so, if that's what his love is like," you snapped, and when I turned away from you I felt your anger rolling over us in waves.

"You never wanted this, Wren. You don't have to for him."

"It's not always bad, Sawyer. It's not."

That wasn't what you wanted to hear. I'm sorry.

I didn't deserve everything that happened to me, good or bad. I'm starting to get that now. You told me so. You were always telling me. But so was he. And it started off slow, and gentle, and then it was too much. I see it now, and it seems so obvious that I can't help but kick myself. But it wasn't then. He knew what he was doing the whole time. He used me. He's always been using me. For what? Because I was easy? Because I am? Because he could?

I'm going to wrap this up because I think I must look like I'm trying not to cry and you look like you're about to stop pretending you don't notice.

I'm so sorry,
Wren

26

Sawyer,

If you're still reading these and haven't come to me about it yet, you've got a stronger stomach than I thought.

Then again, I'm sure you always knew that it was worse than I let on.

But you never thought I'd admit it, did you?

Here's the truth, Sawyer: I've lied to you a lot.

The first time he hit me was right after graduation.

Your parents had spent the entire morning taking pictures of the two of us; both with them, together, individually. Cameron was an afterthought, an insert, an outsider (partially because it wasn't his day, it was ours; and partially, I suspect, because even before things started going really south, I have a feeling your parents didn't like him,). By the time we split off for the ceremony, he was already humming with anger, his skin warm with it. But we were all anxious, and distracted, and I wrote it off. I was already making excuses for him, Sawyer. Please try to understand that. It's so easy to accept things once you've started rationalizing.

We all had plans to meet for dinner – your real family and my weird one and Cam's half one. But it didn't happen. His dad bailed. Your parents tried to remedy the situation by saying we could reschedule. Things fell apart.

He was yelling, and for once I yelled back.

You didn't ask many questions when I came back over that

night. You didn't see the red handprint painted across my cheek because of my ugly blotchy crying face. I didn't tell you he hit me. I just told you it had been a rough night.

Did you know, Sawyer? Did you see it on his face when you talked to me in front of him? Did you feel it in the air when I misspoke?

I didn't tell you, and I believed him when he came begging for forgiveness and wildly, desperately explaining that he would try as hard as he could not to be his father's son.

But he was. I think he could have been someone better, had he been true to his word.

Love, Wren

27

Dearest Sawyer,

Let's start at the beginning, yeah?

Not the very beginning, but the moment that I can definitively pinpoint as the start of the end.

You remember the mounting tension at graduation. The buzz of his discontent rising to a steady hum that drowned out everything else. Him snarling into his phone while your parents and mine stood solemn and poised outside the entrance to the restaurant.

"His dad promised he'd come through this time," I explained, feebly, and I pretended I didn't see you grit your teeth, or your mom shoot a sidelong glance at your dad like they knew something I never would, "he's just really upset. I'm sorry."

It was the apology, I think, that made your dad step forward.

"Cameron," he called, and, because we were in public and he had to maintain some aura of normalcy, Cam swiped his thumb angrily across his screen and then turned toward us, smooth-featured and composed, "we can do this another time. It really doesn't have to be tonight."

"I don't want to spoil everything," Cam said, and every single one of us fell for it, so don't you pretend I was the only one.

"No, you're not spoiling anything," Penny's voice sounded the same as it did when I had first moved in and wouldn't come out of my room – coaxing, comforting, reassuring, "we'll make it work. Tonight, we can go without."

He talked his way out of dinner and talked my way out of it, too, and I kissed your cheek and hugged your parents and told Doug and Penny I'd see them at home. We drove in tentative silence for a few minutes before I dared to speak.

"We could still have dinner with them," I said, and I don't remember how I said it because this was before I learned to always keep my voice light, to always dance around him as though nothing had ever gone wrong.

"It's too late now."

"We could go back to the house. Order in. Make a night of it. It doesn't have to be a total loss."

"Well, sorry I ruined your entire graduation, Wren. I promise you it won't seem like such a monumental deal in the future," he snapped, and I blinked.

"You didn't," I said softly, with more confusion than anything else, "I just meant – "

"Enough! Okay? The night's over."

I didn't point out that clearly it wasn't, because he wasn't driving me home and he wasn't explaining himself.

We pulled into his driveway, and he killed the engine and slammed the door behind him, not waiting to see if I'd follow because he knew that I would. There was nobody else around to contaminate with his frustration, but he made an unnecessary amount of noise anyway, slamming cupboard doors, dropping his feet heavily with each step. I had learned early on in life that it was best to stay out of the way, and so it was hardly an adjustment at all to teach myself to do the same in the face of his anger. It was best to let him work it out of his system on his own, and he'd be back to normal soon enough.

But this was our day. My day. I'd transferred schools six times, shuffled homes, shuffled lives; graduation was no small accomplishment for me, and he was souring it with every footfall.

"Cam, it's not the end of the world. He's always disappointed you."

He waved his hand dismissively at me, using the marble edge of the countertop to snap the cap off a beer.

"What then? Misery loves company? You want me to suffer with you?"

"You could try being a little empathetic, if you're looking for something to do," he challenged, his voice arching as it always did when he was priming for a fight.

"I don't want to argue with you, alright? Not today."

"As opposed to all the other times, when you just can't get enough of it."

"Enough, Cam. Please."

"No, continue. Tell me all about how I've ruined your big night, how I'm bumming you out, how it's such a drag to have to deal with me and my daddy issues."

"Don't put words in my mouth."

"I'm only saying what you won't, aren't I? Because you're not nearly as mean as I am. You'd never tell anyone how you really felt if you thought you'd hurt their feelings – you're nowhere near as nasty as mean old Cameron."

"This was *my day!*" the volume of my voice surprised even me, and I saw his eyebrows dart upward even before he turned to face me, "this was my night, and it was supposed to be fun and celebratory and I've worked hard for this, Cam. I've worked hard for this!"

"It's high school, Wren; you're not going to the moon."

"Easy for you to say when you've had everything *handed* to you your entire life!"

It took me a moment to realize he'd hit me, if I'm honest.

My head spun and my ears rung and I blinked, and then I lifted my hand to my cheek and took a step back.

"Wren – "

"Don't touch me."

"Wren, I'm – "

"*Don't touch me.*"

He pulled his hand back when I spit it the third time, reeling backward and then turning toward the door, racing away as though I expected him to pull me back, panic swelling in my chest.

"Wren, I'm sorry. I'm sorry, please, you don't understand."

"Don't talk to me, and don't touch me, and don't speak to me ever again," I wiped the back of my hand across my nose, growing even angrier at how pathetic my tears must look, how childish to be crying at something so small, "you will *not* lay a single finger on me ever again. Do you understand me? *Never.*"

"You made me angry, I'm sorry, I didn't mean – "

He didn't follow me out the door, but I still ran the whole way to you.

As Always, Wren

28

Sawyer,

  I was tricked into falling for him, but this is how I did.

  After a particularly strenuous week of tests that left the senior class of Clearwell High in a state of dazed self-loathing, we all made our way to Ochlockonee.

  He dragged his feet a little, making vague comments about irresponsible high schoolers and bad decisions and feeling out of his element, but at this point he was still working hard to win everyone over and couldn't put up too much of a fight without risking it.

  I rode with him, much to your dismay, reassuring him ten times over that I had no interest in drinking and that you didn't either; he still treated you like a person, back then, and you were capable of civil conversation. We found a bonfire and a group of friends, sipped Coke from glass bottles and picked the golden crusts off roasted marshmallows until our fingers were sticky and sweet. Everyone was light with the relief of the week being over, with the company of each other, with the soft night air and stars twinkling through the branches overhead. I laughed so hard that I leaned into the people around me and felt it in my veins, the two of us entertaining the crowd with wild stories and coaxing lazy grins out of Cam. I kicked off my shoes and wriggled my toes in the sand. People screeched and cannonballed into the water somewhere in the shadows. You dragged a whole cooler out of your car and flung ice into the fire to watch it dance. We were lightweight and so unbelievably young.

As the night went on and sleepy students climbed back into vehicles to head home, we all shifted closer together around the shrinking fire, elbows and hips and ankles touching, the night closing in on us. There was music playing in the darkness nearby, people murmuring and laughing around the other two fires. You made a big show of stretching and yawning, hooking your ankle through mine when you stood to announce your departure.

I followed you to your car, standing beside you in the one-AM stillness and the damp chill of the air.

"Is it okay?" I asked, and you kept your head bowed as you fitted your cooler into the passenger seat, waiting to answer.

This was the first time you were leaving this place without me since we'd met, the first time you'd come alone. I could see it in the curve of your spine in retrospect, the *no it's not okay Sparrow but I don't know why*, the reluctance.

"Yeah, Wren," you said, standing straight and then pressing a kiss to the top of my head, "it's fine."

I waited until your taillights disappeared from view before I made my way back over to the fire, where the group was rolling at something Cam was saying. I settled down next to him and let my knee brush his, lifting my bottle from where it rested between us and taking a slow sip. His hand lingered on the small of my back, his eyes twinkling in the firelight.

"Everything okay with Sawyer?" he asked, and even knowing what I know now, he still sounded like he actually cared.

"Yeah, he's just tired. Long week for all of us," I tried not to let my gaze linger too long on the space where you'd been; he'd asked about us before, and I didn't want to give him any reason to ask again.

My hair smelled like wood smoke and my skin was blue in

the moonlight, and the air was the kind of cool that makes your lungs feel weightless. I wriggled my bare toes in the sand and leaned in toward the fire, though I was already acutely aware of the heat from Cam crossing the half-inch of space between us and seeping into my bones. My heart still pounded in my throat every time he was near me, still raced at every point of contact. The night swam around us and fitted itself into the hollows of our throats.

I don't really remember how it happened. I don't remember most of it. I do remember his voice from the end of a tunnel, my name muted and sticking to the roof of his mouth, his hand on my elbow.

"Wren, are you okay?"

My eyes flitting unsteadily, my body swaying like I was walking a tightrope despite the fact that I was still sitting down.

"Don't feel so good," my words came out in an unintelligible jumble, most of them staying somewhere in my throat.

"Are you sick? Hey, look at me," I tried to find his face, but there were too many of them swirling around me, and I wasn't sure which one was really his, "what did you drink?"

I just wanted to lie down, my limbs leaden and my head lurching inside itself. He pulled his keys out of his pocket, the rustle distorted and deafening as he flashed his penlight in my eyes.

"Don't," I tried to throw my hand up, but only managed a weak wave, nearly falling backward off the log in the process.

"Who touched her drink?" he was so angry. His voice hammered on the inside of my skull, his rage hot under my skin, "who *touched her drink?*"

There were no volunteers, obviously, and he kept his hand steady against my side the entire time, scooping me up as though I weighed nothing at all and speaking soothing words I couldn't understand when I protested weakly at the rapid swirling of the earth beneath us.

"I'm sorry, but I need you to," and I could feel his finger pressing at the back of my tongue, his other hand knotting my hair back from my face as I wretched into the bushes by his car, leaning heavily against him. Somehow, I was on the ground, the dirt packed cold and hard beneath me, the headlights of leaving vehicles dazzling and blinding all at once.

Maybe that's why I can remember anything at all. But it's the last thing I remember until I woke up to the sky turning pink, the taste of acid and sand on my tongue and in an unfamiliar room.

I didn't even have time to panic. I still felt bleary - exhausted and disoriented and sluggish, nausea brewing in the pit of my stomach – but he was waiting on a kitchen chair at my side, a glass of water on the bedside table, ready to explain my fears away.

So boy meets girl. Boy drugs girl. Boy brings girl home, takes care of her, tells her he saved her from a far more terrifying fate.

Girl falls in love, sharply and fearfully and for all the wrong reasons.

Love you most,
Wren

29

Sawyer,

About five months after we started dating, Cam and I ran into one of his old friends.

It's clear in retrospect, knowing all his tics and microscopic mannerisms, that Cam was not excited to see him. But in the moment, I didn't know. He was all pearly-whites and back-clapping hugs, introducing me with a grandiose sweep of his arm.

Tom had been on the hockey team all the way through college, he explained, though I could have guessed from the way his dark hair was swept back from his face and curled around his ears. He had perfect teeth in a slightly lopsided mouth, and a mischievous twinkle in his eye that didn't seem to need a source.

Basically, he was gorgeous, which you may (incorrectly) assume was why Cam would be guarded.

"I should've known Cam would end up with someone like you after all the rest," Tom said later, after coffees and desserts and lazy reminiscing, "he needed someone to settle him down."

"Sounds like he was already pretty settled when we met," I laughed, and Cam flinched almost imperceptibly at it – I wasn't yet practiced in faking nonchalance, and our length conversation had unveiled a lot about who Cam had been, regardless of whether or not he had realized it (he had).

Even in high school, Cam had been someone who was used to getting what he wanted. They went to that gated, private school almost half an hour north; and they ruled it, eventually.

I'm sure I received only the most golden-edged versions of their escapades, but the gist I got as that in a music montage of their teen years, Cam and Tom and their hockey boys would have sauntered down the halls in slow-motion, smirking in the general direction of guys who stared enviously from the corners of their eyes and girls who swooned as they passed by.

They were royalty, reckless and haughty and magnetic. They threw parties that sent ripples through the lives of their peers and never saw a shadow of the backlash. Friends in high places, and all that. Friends who provided their own forms of entertainment and also letters of recommendation for Cam's future career path.

"He burned his way through half the girls at school and half the interns at the hospital before he even had his foot in the door," Tom had a ghost of nostalgia in the way that he spoke, like maybe things didn't all still fall into place so easily.

"He's exaggerating," Cam rolled his eyes, shooting a look across the table, "and besides, we were kids. Stupid kids."

"Not that stupid," Tom mused, leaning back in his chair and winking, "we never got caught."

They truly believed that the life they'd lead – the life they'd created for themselves and the people around them – was harmless. That the reason they no longer lived it was not because it was dangerous and destructive but because it was unsustainable. But they never stopped to see the disasters left in their wake – girls who carried stun guns and never again went out alone, boys who lost track of time and sometimes fell out of it all together.

So as you can see, Sawyer, it was not that they were malicious. It was that the world had only ever wronged those who deserved it, and they had somehow managed to stay in its good graces.

They were spoiled, neglected by their parents and punished erratically. Pitied by teachers who let things slide too far and too often – because how were they to know? Everything they had, they'd made for themselves – but only because nobody had ever paid enough attention to tell them that they couldn't.

The reason that Cam was weary about my meeting Tom was not even because he revealed a side of him that he had worked hard to either overcome or conceal. It was that he thought I might see his past in our present.

It was that he saw himself – this new, manicured version of Cameron – in the gleam in Tom's eye that had never faded with age. And it scared him; the idea that he could have become someone so glossy and renewed, and still be exactly the same at his core.

Because Cam knew, Sawyer. Maybe not at the beginning, maybe not when he was fifteen and still had his mom at home to reel him back in. But when she left – when she realized that there is only so much that a person can give of herself before it is too much – he knew, then. He knew that the world shifts around the things we say and do, and it only made him more dangerous. Those girls who accepted drinks from boys they trusted and woke up different people, those boys who still to this day cannot quite catch up to that rush they're craving; they're all casualties in the game Cam started and never stopped playing. He may have walked away relatively unscathed, but, clearly, he never once loosened his hold on the reins.

The only thing Cam learned from turning into his father was that he had to be a prettier monster than Ed was.

Of course, I didn't realize all of this then, and I didn't realize it all at once. It came in bits and pieces – Tom emailing me at work, the young women from their yearbooks telling their stories on their social media accounts and all but naming names. He was never directly involved, of course – but his fingerprints were all over those circles just as they were all over my life.

All these years later, sitting across the table from someone who had become his past only because he was too much of an open book, and the only thing that had changed about Cam was the steadiness of his hand.

Maybe he knew all along,
Wren

30

My Other Half,

I think a lot about real, actual love, and what it feels like.

I know what it doesn't.

But Sawyer, I think both of us also know how it does.

It feels like the moment that your eyes meet in a crowd and the band around your lungs breaks free. It feels like the warmth spreading up your wrist when your knuckles brush in passing. It feels like comfortable silences, and laughter breaking through your skin, and understanding.

Even though we've always been together, Sawyer, you're still the one that got away. We both are, aren't we? Not geographically, not physically. We're both the ones that got away, because though we've always had each other, though, technically, we could still get back to where we were, something will always stand in our way. Mentally, emotionally, we will never be what we could.

I am so much better for having known you, and I really wish and hope that sometimes you can say the same for me.

I wondered, for awhile, if that was why he couldn't love me the right way. Because I couldn't anymore, either.

I don't blame myself anymore. I try not to, at least. I did wonder if it started because he always felt that he was second place to you, and then his hatred and his anger and his violence made his fears a self-fulfilling prophecy.

But you don't tell someone about your insecurities with

your fists and your teeth and your rage.

I don't know how to explain it to you in a way that will make you understand. I don't think it's possible for you to know, unless you've been there. But his loathing for me worked its way under my skin disguised as love, and by the time he really started hitting me, it made sense. I talked back, I raised my voice, I fought him when all he wanted to do was help. I made him turn into the monster he had always feared he would, and for that, I owed him. I owed him what he would never get from anyone else, after what I had made of him.

I owed him love, and respect, and my penance. I deserved to hate myself as much as he did.

Because I never told you about the first time that he hit me, you didn't experience the escalation. What's that saying, about the difference between jumping into boiling water or just feeling the warmth grow? That night in your dorm room, with my eyes glazed over and my teeth stained crimson, you saw a massive leap from the controlling and cranky Cameron that you'd slowly grown to resent. You couldn't understand why I was on the defensive, why I didn't spit out the taste of his name. For you, this was the breaking point of what had previously been nothing but an unstable and loud relationship. For me, it was just a misstep.

You didn't know that I'd apologized for provoking him, that first afternoon when the back of his hand had left shame simmering on my cheekbone. You didn't know that I believed, truly and completely, that it had been what he needed.

It's a cycle, Sawyer, and he was never going to break it if I didn't help him.

That's what he told me, and so that's what I told myself.

And I know, now, I know that even if you had seen it, if I'd told you right from the start – of course you wouldn't have felt the same way that I did. Of course you wouldn't have been able to justify it the way that I did, that he did.

There were bright days – vivid and sharp in my memory. Days when I laughed so hard it hurt, when I wasn't afraid, when I could see who he was meant to be. Those days gave me hope, and when my hope started to fade, so did they, until they were worn soft at the edges from turning them over in my mind. When I was too tired to keep helping him, he was too tired to try, and eventually the exhaustion overtook both of us.

Tiredly yours,
Wren

31

Sawyer,

By the time it clicked, it was too late.

I was too far in, too far gone, too smoothed down and glazed over and desynchronized.

Even if I hadn't been, I didn't know who to go to. I didn't even know what I would tell someone if I did. Or I did, but some part of me knew even then that it was futile.

I couldn't tell you. I'm sorry. It's not your fault. None of this is your fault.

Maybe it was because I'd dragged him along back down to the bay when he'd made it clear that he didn't want to go. Maybe it was that he knew you'd be there and so he didn't want me to go alone, but I'd told you I'd be there, and that made him feel obligated. He didn't want to be the bad guy.

I always made him be the bad guy.

But he seemed fine. Fine enough that you gave my shoulder a gentle squeeze as you ducked away to say hi to some newly arriving friends. Fine enough that your space was quickly filled in by stragglers and acquaintances, all itching for him to rain some charm down on them, all vying for a small beam of his warmth.

He's always had that draw. I'd know.

And I didn't know it yet. I hadn't seen it yet. I didn't realize how deliberate every move was, how unfaltering he had always been. Rarely did I catch him off guard, and when I did it was always with the result of enough vitriol to deter me from doing it again.

(That was intentional too, of course.)

Somebody else brought it up, not him. He would have been counting on the faltering, on the side-eyed caution following the mention of any recreational drug use in front of a professional, in front of someone far more adult than us.

And he grinned, reached into his pocket. Extracted a small sandwich baggie of pills illuminated gold and blue and red in the firelight.

A flick of the wrist, a catch, the evidence vanishing into the shadows of some nameless, faceless boy.

"Have at it," that grin that makes your knees go weak, your heart swell with pride for having earned it, "I've got my use of them."

It didn't click. It didn't click. I grabbed his wrist, stood on my tiptoes so that he would turn his ear toward my lips.

"You'll lose your job if anyone hears about this," I warned him through blind panic, though that shouldn't have been the first thought in my head, in my heart, "you'd lose everything, or – "

And he laughed. He laughed and he threw his arm around my neck, pulling me close and kissing my hairline roughly.

"It's fine, kiddo. Don't worry about it."

We didn't go back to the bay much after that. Eventually it was almost like I'd dreamt it.

I mentioned it once, weeks later, and he shut me down with such nonchalance and ease, eyes dark, that I never brought it up again.

That's usually how things went with Cam.

You don't understand, do you Sawyer? You don't know why I didn't speak up, why I didn't run, why I just stood there and did nothing.

I wish I had answers for you. But I don't. Everything made so much sense, at the time.

Love,
The Great Love of Your Life

32

Sawyer Moore,

    Considering how quick I had been to cut him off, you're undoubtedly wondering how I was almost quicker to go back to him.

    You have to keep in mind, Sawyer, that hindsight is 20/20, and that things seem a lot more obvious in anyone's shoes but my own.

    I came home from work – remember our summer job at the pool where we spent more time in the water than actually working at all – and he was sitting on the porch steps, arms crossed at the wrist on his knees, looking exhausted and thoroughly pitiful. It had been two weeks without so much as a word from him, and I'd been alright with it. You'd been thrilled, but you'd tried not to show it (and to anyone else, you'd have been convincing).

    He looked up when I stopped at the end of the lawn, jaw clenched and shoulders back, leveling him with the coldest stare I could manage when my heart was pounding in my chest.

    I'd spent hours mentally playing with how things would go the next time I ran into him – this was not any of the scenarios. He'd caught me off guard (intentionally, and for more than one reason). I was still damp and smelled of sweat and sunscreen, my hair curling around my face and my sundress clinging to my swimsuit unevenly.

    "You need to leave," I sounded far steadier than I felt, but he was unshaken, rising to his feet, "you need to get out of here right now. I told Penny and Doug. They'll be home and when they see you they'll call the police."

"If you'd told them, they already would have," he called my bluff instantaneously and without any indication of remorse, "but you didn't, and I have to believe that means you're still willing to at least talk to me."

"I pity you," I spit, "because you think you're worth any of our concern."

He actually looked hurt by this, and I felt my first pang of guilt.

"I messed up, Wren. I know I did. Please let me explain."

"There's no explanation. You hit me."

"I know. I'm sorry. If you give me another chance – "

"Another chance? So there can be a next time? So there can be a last time?"

"No. So *that* can be the last time. The only time. Wren, I promise, if you'll just hear me out, I'll leave you alone. I just need you to understand so that you can have closure."

"So that *you* can, more like."

"That too. Please? I'll buy you coffee. We can take a walk. I won't touch you. There's so much I haven't told you."

Be quiet, but don't make yourself a target. Be yielding, but not easy. Be forgiving, but not illogical. Listen when it is asked of you.

"I'll buy my own coffee, thanks."

Clearwell is a small town, and so you feel safe. But you also feel exposed, because everyone knows nearly everything about you and thinks they know the rest. There is a strange sense of loyalty between the members of the community, often about the absolute worst things to be protective of.

There is no way in hell nobody knew about Ed Stone

beating his wife and son.

I know he's a liar. I know he manipulates, and he twists the truth, and he promises things he has no intention of keeping. I know that, now. But then, he was just a boy I loved, telling me about losing his mother and being left with his monster alcoholic father.

There were signs already, but I was blind to them.

He cried when he told me. Maybe some of it was real. I find it hard to explain now without shedding doubt on it, because now I know and then I didn't. That's my truth.

Ed had been drunk and disorderly for as long as Cam could remember. Drunk and disorderly in a very calculated way, of course, considering the complete lack of evidence to anyone who didn't go looking (and why would they? He was the sheriff, after all). He would come home from work, and it would start with a beer while he detached himself from the day. Then two. Then three. A glass of wine with Cam's mom at dinner, a glass of whiskey as he sat down at the TV.

It was mostly grumblings and silences, falling asleep in his chair with an empty bottle in his hand; but there were explosions, screaming eruptions that made nine-year-old Cam cower in his bedroom closet and wish the neighbors were closer. The older he got, the louder the fights became, and then Cam realized it had been a long time since they were just noise.

There were times he was caught in the middle, times he was used as a pawn by both sides. And then there was the time he put himself there, and she left.

"I thought I was helping her," he told me, snot-nosed and bleary-eyed, cradling his head in his hands and keeping a good foot of space between us even though his entire body leaned toward mine as though it wanted nothing more than to close the gap, "I thought I could protect her."

I didn't speak, and it was because all I could do to keep from crying myself was to keep my teeth clenched tight and my arms folded across my chest, gripping my own elbows.

"I was sixteen, and finally about as tall as him. He'd cornered her; he liked to make her think she had a chance to get out of it before he'd really lay into her. But I couldn't just sit there. I don't know what it was. That time wasn't any different from the others, but maybe it had just been building up to this moment."

He waited for a moment, like he was expecting a response, but when I said nothing he continued, slowly.

"I got in his way, like I did sometimes, but I squared off. He thought it was funny until I hit him."

The match nearly ended with her bringing both of them to the ER. Of course, Ed talked her out of it. But when Cam woke up the next morning, his mom was gone, nothing missing but an armful of clothing and her purse, and she'd never contacted either of them again.

"I thought he was lying to me for awhile. That maybe he'd killed her. Or even that she had run away, but was trying to get in touch and he was blocking her, somehow. But she's alive. Living in Washington. She just left me behind. Has a husband and two daughters who probably don't even know about me."

The tightness in my chest snapped, and I found myself reaching for his hand, my fingers grazing his.

"She was afraid of me, too," he said tearfully, "to her, I had just become a smaller version of him."

Round and round and round.

He was pathetic, and I don't mean that harshly. But he was so heartbroken, so genuine that I couldn't help but believe every word he said.

I'm not making excuses for myself. But he pleaded. He promised never to be that version of himself again. He promised to be better.

And he was, for awhile.

Love, Wren

33

Dearest Darling Sawyer,

It was like finally telling somebody opened a spout from the recesses of Cam's brain. He'd call me in the middle of the night, asking gently if we could talk and then beginning while I was still wiping the sleep from my eyes and pulling the blanket over my head to muffle the sound of my voice. Sometimes I'd arrive home from work to find him waiting, looking humbled and almost shy, with coffee or iced tea or individually wrapped treats.

I didn't tell you, because I knew what you'd say. That alone should have been an indication.

Once he'd eased my guard down, he started pressing harder. Our walks would lead back to his house, where I'd say goodbye at the sidewalk, and then the porch, and then the door. Two months after graduation, I turned to leave and he pulled me back, allowing me one moment of hesitation before pressing his lips to mine. I pushed away after what he seemed to deem an appropriate pause, because after that he always kissed me goodbye.

Three more weeks of that before you caught on, and that was only because you caught *me*.

"Is that a *hickey?*" the disbelief in your voice was almost enough to make me laugh in spite of the instant panic it invoked. You grabbed my shoulders (this was back when you still treated me like I was made of flesh and bones instead of china) and swept my hair back from my neck in one motion, gasping in exaggerated shock when your suspicions were confirmed.

"Shut up," I pushed you off, tugging my hair back around my throat and hunching my shoulders.

"I've gotta say, Sparrow. I'm hurt. Clearly you've got a man and clearly it's not me."

"Shut *up,*" I repeated, and though I tried to sound like I was joking, you frowned at the sudden change in tone.

"Please don't tell me it's who I think it is."

I ignored you, smoothing invisible wrinkles out of my shirt.

"Wren Jones, do you know what you're doing?"

You'd have put up more of a fight, had you known. I know that. It's why I didn't tell you.

"Don't you let him do anything you don't want to do," you made me look at you, bowing your head so our foreheads touched, locking eyes with me, "and don't you do anything rash."

"Well, you'd be a fine judge of that, wouldn't you?" I retorted, just as softly, and you smirked ever so slightly.

"Seriously though, Sparrow," you head-butted me gently, standing up, "don't you ever accept anything less than you deserve. And that's the best, by the way."

"It's fine. I'm just taking it slow. Figuring out where we stand."

I thought about that while his hands slid up the back of my shirt and I pushed them back down. I thought about it when he pinned me in the corner, stamping kisses up my neck and sliding his palms across my hipbones. I thought about it every time I said no, and every time I pushed back, and then I thought about it when I didn't say or do anything at all.

I thought about it when I heard your car roll up behind me, still wearing yesterday's clothes and yesterday's makeup, my skin too tight and too thin and too exposed.

"I thought you were waiting," you said, and in my head I thought *so did I.*

I'm still waiting,
Wren

34

Sawyer,

When I moved into my first apartment, I didn't feel stuck.

It was small; two rooms and a bathroom, with the coffee table an arm's length from the tiny stove and an entryway so minuscule it could hardly contain a single pair of sandals.

But it was light, and the floors were soft-worn wood, and the windowsills were wide enough to house my endless train of plants until we could build them proper shelves.

I wasn't allowed to paint, so you surprised me with armfuls of dyed and patterned fabrics that we tacked strategically to the walls of our choice. We played alternative music at a respectable volume so as to not disturb my new neighbors, and you built me bookshelves narrow enough to fit in the space between my windows and doors.

Together we unpacked; all of my belongings fit easily into the back of your dad's pickup truck, and even more easily into my new home. When we'd finished, we invited our parents to see our handiwork, and they mused as they stood shoulder-to-chest-to-elbow that the space was perfect for the two of us, since it was only big enough for one. You made us dinner. We ate off of new plates with new cutlery and watched movies with our legs intertwined at the knee.

After setting up my small desk fan and tugging the curtains shut tight, I slept in my own bed in my own apartment. Everything I saw was mine. Everything I touched was mine. Even you, knocking on the door and then entering of your own accord with bags full of baking supplies: you were mine.

It was too small for Cam's liking; he was adjusted to wide spaces and high ceilings and windows that all opened outward.

But it was better that way, wasn't it? Even if I didn't know it at the time.

That was the last year we really had together, wasn't it? And even then, by the end we were tearing at the seams.

You'd pull up behind our friends at red lights and stop signs, rev your engine and laugh at the fire in my eyes. We spent weekends driving too fast on back roads where the Spanish moss hung thick and made light-speckled tunnels, the snarl of your engine and the ease of your hands on the gearshift riling me up until I'd pull the sunroof back and climb up, stretching my arms skyward and shouting over the sound of your laughter. When it was just us, we were invincible.

We showed up everywhere wind-whipped and leaning into each other, your hands still smelling faintly of oil and my skin swept tight with salty air.

It was the last summer of the "little retro place" being only that. Back when we still were seen together in public. Back before our friends crumbled away and the only ones left were those willing avert their eyes.

It was inexpensive, and strangely comfortable, lit in strips of pink and blue neon and decorated with aging tiles. The two of us and whichever members of our crew decided to tag along that day would cram into the same corner, spilling into the surrounding seats and taking over the diner with our light.

You were so effortless in everything that you did, swinging your long limbs as you climbed over me to fit yourself against the wall, connecting us from shoulder-to-hip-to-ankle until you stretched your arm along the bench behind us and made space for me to lean back against your chest.

How many milkshakes have we shared, and salt-crusted plates of flawlessly greasy fries? Too many to count, and yet never enough.

I haven't gone in it without you, and someday we'll go again. Maybe it'll still feel the same. A girl can dream, right?

Right? Wren

35

The Great Love of My Life,

There are a lot of ways to tell someone you love them without actually speaking the words.

"Drive safe. Text me when you get there."

"Let me know if you need anything."

"I'll take care of it."

Sometimes you show it, absently or unintentionally, with habits or actions that turn into them. Like how you always use the big red mug when you make me hot chocolate because you know that it's my favorite. Or how you skip over scenes in movies that have a lot of yelling. You know things. You see things. You say, "you can stay here tonight."

The first time I showed up at your door, your freshman year in your tiny little matchbox of a dorm room, I thought for sure I'd ruined us. There was something in your eyes like I was the last person you wanted to see; but really it was that you just didn't want to see me *like that*. I kept apologizing while you gently wiped the blood from the crease of my upper lip and checked my eyes for signs of concussion. Your roommate cursed a lot and paced until you gave him a look and he ducked out.

"Did he do this to you?" you asked, and you were so *angry*, Sawyer.

"It was an accident – "

"*Did he do this to you*, Wren?" and you kicked your

bedframe and ran your hand over your face like it physically pained you to exist in that moment, "so, what? Pushing you around wasn't enough? He had a little more work to do before he got you fully brainwashed?"

You know what you said. I'm not repeating it to make you regret it – I know you did the second it was out of your mouth. But you were right, and I didn't give you a choice but to ignore that.

I flinched when you turned around, and you nearly cried. I pretended I didn't see, because otherwise you would have. But instead, you got an ice pack from your freezer, and wrapped it in one of your t-shirts, and held it to the darkening bruise under my left eye while I rested my head on your shoulder.

I slept in your XL twin dorm bed that night, curled up in one of your hoodies and a pair of your sweatpants. I buried myself in your smell and your warmth and I tried to tell myself that I wasn't really going to go back to him this time. You sat diligently with me the whole night, smoothing my hair back from my face and breathing slow and steady. I heard you whisper, almost inaudibly, "I wish I knew how to help you."

You saved me every day, Sawyer.

In the morning, your roommate brought us breakfast and we ate it in silence sitting cross-legged on your couch, turned so that our knees touched and neither of us could see my reflection in the mirror on your closet door.

"Stay one more night," you said first, and I didn't respond, and we stayed in heavy but still familiar silence until I gathered myself up and grabbed my keys.

And when I was leaving, "be careful," when my hand was on the door handle but couldn't quite seem to turn it, "you're always welcome here."

I wish I had stayed. I wish I had run away then. I know now. I do. And I can see it in your face right here and now as you watch me from behind the hood of the truck you're working on, your hands streaked with grease and grit – you don't think that I do. I come to you on Thursdays when he's gone late and I have time to watch you work, because you think that I don't see what he's made of me, and you still love me, anyway.

I do still love you too,
Wren

36

Sawyer,

    Having grown up nowhere near the tropical vibes of your hometown, it took me awhile to adjust to your ease.

    Or rather, it took me awhile to match it.

    We'd get looks whenever we'd come into a room together, either because we entered as one tangled windblown laughing unit, or because of the effortlessness of every movement – you sweeping the door open and me ducking under your arm as you fell in line behind me. It was easy for everyone to see that we fit together like halves of a whole – it was just harder for them to comprehend it being just that.

    For most of my life I'd avoided physical contact like the plague despite craving it; even feeling the warmth from someone sitting close by was enough to send me from the room. But with you it was constant and subtle and natural – my legs hooked over yours whenever we sat, your hand grazing the bones of my wrist and flitting over the small of my back as you passed by. I'd shift just enough for my elbow to nudge yours as I slipped through a doorway, lean in a little bit too far so our shoulders would brush – feel the warmth simmering in my bones where you'd been. Since we had nearly immediately done away with the need for personal space and become accustomed to each other's quirks, I wasn't testing you, but rather egging you on – encouraging the elimination of space between us, volunteering to do it myself.

    Once we got past the reluctance to talk about what we were,

things fell into place quicker and with faultless ease. Kisses on cheeks and foreheads and the spaces above our ears became greetings and farewells; I fitted myself against your side effortlessly with no prompt but the lift of your arm to welcome me in. You'd drop your chin into the curve of my shoulder or rest your hand knotted at the nape of my neck. We were connected by invisible wires that tugged us back together whenever we strayed too far. Anything else was incomprehensible.

That hasn't gone anywhere. Even when the space between us is carefully measured and mandated, I still notice your ring finger trailing across my wrist when you step past, still see that your knees angle toward mine and that your heart is always pointed in my direction. I see you. I know.

When I get out, I'll come back for that – I can't take you with me and risk everything that we are – I'm sorry. You'll know where to find me. We're in this together, even though I wish with all my heart that you wouldn't be.

I'm sorry,
Wren

37

Wonderful, Wonderful Sawyer,

In the middle of August 2009, my landlord informed me that my rent would be increasing by upwards of *way too much money for someone like me to ever be able to afford.*

You had just left again for your second year of college, after many late-night conversations on your front porch about whether or not you should go at all. I'd reassured you (lying through my teeth all the while) that he hadn't laid a finger on me since I'd shown up at your dorm the last time, and that you staying wouldn't have changed anything even if he had. In the end you dropped out halfway through the year anyway, so maybe you staying could have thrown a wrench in the way things went after all, but I digress.

I didn't call you after the meeting with my landlord. I knew what you'd say – that you'd help, that your parents or mine would board me, that we'd figure something out. But in spite of feeling more at home with my parents than I could have ever imagined I would, I couldn't bring myself to force myself back into their home after I'd given them the satisfaction of raising me out of it. I was never your parents' responsibility. And, Sawyer, I was never yours.

Cam was, obviously, the one to suggest that I start renting the ground-level room at his house. It made sense, the way he phrased it – the back door was only a few feet away, so I could come and go as I pleased. I'd have my own bathroom just down the stairs. Rent would be manageable, and I could help around the house in lieu of paying for utilities. I balked at the idea at first – still holding tight to my own long-term personal beliefs despite his determination to dissolve them entirely – but he insisted, seeming increasingly hurt each time I suggested that he help me find my own place instead.

I still didn't tell you. I never told you when I did things I knew would make the light in your eyes flicker and the corners of your mouth twitch downward. I never told you when I did anything that you knew I didn't want to, because arguing with you was even worse than arguing with myself, especially when you were right.

I didn't renew my lease, and I moved into his spare room at the beginning of September.

At first it was fine. I tidied up around the house when I wasn't at work, and he always waited for a response before entering after he knocked. I handed him checks for rent each month, crisp and neatly printed. He made space for my things on the shelves in the living room, and parked to the side so that my car could fit beside his. Things started slow.

By the end of October he was rapping his knuckles against the doorframe as he pushed it open, catching me half-dressed or wrapped in a towel or just unprepared, laughing (though not meanly, not yet) when I would shout out in indignation, and oftentimes I would find myself fighting back a smile myself at the apologetic look on his face, the insistence that he hadn't meant to, that he didn't mind if I didn't. He'd be waiting up when I came home late, trailing his fingers around the rim of his glass and casting suspicious looks at the glow on my skin. I started checking my watch more frequently, changing in the bathroom.

At the start of November, he pushed too hard in response to my reluctance, raising his voice and demanding an explanation for why I insisted on keeping to myself when we lived together anyway

He mocked my skewed moral system and slammed his bedroom door, later coming to try and make it up to me and finding me wrapped in so many layers of clothing that he would have needed an excavator to try and find his idea of forgiveness. By the end of the month, I had been admitted for the first time, and by the time I was back in the house my bedroom had been relocated to his and it turned out my reservations had never mattered to him anyway. By January you were home for good, and I started staying late so that I could slip home in the night when the odds of him having already fallen asleep were higher.

I told you everything was fine. I told you the hospital visit was a fluke and that he was helping me get better. You knew I was lying, but instead of fighting me on it you gave me a safe place to land.

You stopped resisting so much when I'd tell you that it wasn't always bad, and I know now that you only did it to keep me close, because you couldn't help me at all if I cut you off.

It became normal to me. I think it became normal to you, too, though I know you never liked a single second of it. But we ate breakfast and dinner together and watched movies and passed each other in the hall, and he made me laugh. I adapted. I promise you; it wasn't always bad.

I promise,
Wren

38

Sawyer Sawyer Sawyer,

In January of 2010, when you had officially decided that you were not going back to school (and insisted, with no evidence to back it up, that it was not because of me) and were renting an apartment in town, I spent a brisk afternoon in your bedroom, sprawled across the side of your bed closest to the wall heating unit. You were assembling shelves and ignoring the directions, and I was flipping channels because even with cable your television was useless entertainment.

I somehow ended up on a documentary about a dead woman, murdered and disposed of by her husband. The show focused on traumatic bonding: how she felt indebted to the same man who killed her. You made a comment about watching something so dark, but you didn't change the channel. It wasn't until two years later that I woke in the night, heart racing, with the footage zipping through my head. It hit me, suddenly, that it was only going to get worse from here, and I wasn't going to see it until it was too late.

But, I convinced myself: everything seems worse in the middle of the night.

I spent my breaks in the office surfing the web for info on things like Stockholm Syndrome and gaslighting; I made diagrams in my head of all the "I never said that"s and the constant and unpredictable personality changes. It had come to a point where I was starting to spend more time on my toes than not, and with each new

Cameron that emerged I grew wearier. Two years gives you a lot of time to resent someone.

But it also gives you a lot of time to make excuses for them.

With Cam in my head, my diagrams were overthought, dramatic, exaggerated. I heard him wrong – he didn't misspeak. He didn't lie – he had never said it at all. If he were *really* abusive, wouldn't I know, not just wonder? Wouldn't everyone else know, as well? If he were *really* abusive, if this were *really* not the way things should be, wouldn't somebody else have stepped in and told me?

I know you did,
Wren

39

Sawyer,

    I don't know if all parents do this or just fosters, but I learned how to swim by force.

    When I was seven, and briefly in the care of the Turner family, I had a pool.

    It was everything my little heart could have imagined – there was a fountain, and a diving board, and an entire shed filled with inflatable rings and foam tubes and diving toys. Their biological children - both several years older than me and openly skeptical about my existence in their house – were gifted swimmers; I'd watch from the edge as they flipped and dove and raced each other from end to end. Nobody pushed me to get in the water – not at first, at least – but even at that age I could tell that they couldn't quite wrap their heads around my resistance. Even their parents swam. I'd change into the suit they bought me, wrap myself in one of their obscenely oversized beach towels, and perch on the wooden porch steps, watching with jealous fascination.

    They obviously couldn't risk their foster child drowning on their watch. There was a brief conversation about teaching me in the shallow end, my foster siblings splashing around in exaggerated examples, but when I politely declined, the mood changed. Mr. Turner simply strolled over to me, scooped me up in one arm, and flung me into the deepest water, watching with folded arms as I came up retching.

Nobody has ever seemed horrified when I've told them this story, which leads me to believe that it's at least passably normal. But for seven-year-old Wren, this was the ultimate betrayal. I can still feel the water burning in the back of my nose, my lungs, still taste the blood on my tongue as I wildly kicked my way to the edge and held tight to the hot concrete patio. They watched as I hauled myself out of the water with toothpick arms (I had just recently been given a clean bill of health from the doctors who had spent the first years of my life fixing the many physical and psychological problems that came with being a NAS baby of unknown origin, but I was still almost alarmingly thin for some time to come), and crumpled, soaked and shivering, on the pavement. Even I, my own worst critic, know that I must have been a truly pathetic sight to behold; snot nosed and hiccupping and confused.

"Take a deep breath," he said, not unkindly, kneeling down so he was close to my level when I sat up, "calm down, Wren."

So I did, and he tossed me in again.

I know (or at least would like to believe) that if I had shown actual inability to keep myself afloat, someone would have grabbed me. At the time, though? I was convinced that they were going to let me drown – Mrs. Turner with one hand resting on each now-silent child's heads as I paddled my way to the ladder, shimmied my way out, and nearly immediately found myself splashing back in.

Finally, tired of getting chlorine up my nose and down my throat and in my eyes, I admitted defeat, weakly but rhythmically jerking my limbs in some twig-legged imitation of treading water. And that, apparently, was what they had wanted all along; once I stopped trying to escape and simply focused on keeping myself afloat, the entire family cheered and I was welcomed out of the water into open arms and a towel the size of a blanket.

(This is messed up, right? Am I the only one who thinks this is messed up?)

Anyway, all of this comes to mind for a situation that undoubtedly is, half a lifetime later in the Gulf of Mexico.

It was probably the fourth or fifth time we had been out on the boat. I had grown significantly more comfortable, letting my feet dangle over the edge under the railing on the bow and even taking my life vest off when the water was smooth (I know, I know).

So let's set the scene: I was standing at the tallest point of the boat – not a place really made to be stood on, but somewhere I had found I liked to be, regardless. The sky was clear, and the water was lapping softly at the sides and there wasn't another soul in sight. We had argued briefly, in the car on the way to the docks; he didn't want to do anything for Christmas, and our parents had invited him to join the rest of us in our usual festivities. I was frustrated – knowing even then that if I went without him, I'd be hearing about it for days, but if I spent the day with him instead I'd hear about that, too. We hadn't yet come to an agreement, but by the time we were out on the water we both seemed to have come to at least a temporary truce. If he was still stewing (he was), then I was oblivious to it (unsurprising, at that point).

It happened so suddenly and so quickly that it almost seemed to be a mistake – even when I first broke the surface, gasping, and my salt-bleary eyes connected with his vacant ones.

Reeling, still stunned, I paddled back toward him, my fingers slipping on the wet metal as I made surprised little sputtering noises.

"Give me a hand?" I asked, almost joking, almost still believing, despite the look on his face, that it was an accident.

"Can you tread water?" he asked, after a pause two beats too long, still making no move to grab my scrabbling hands.

"Barely," my heart was pounding in my throat so forcefully now that I imagined a beacon pulsing through the sea, *fresh blood right here, still pumping*!

"You never take your life vest off in open water," he leaned forward, but made no move to extend a hand, "even if you're a strong swimmer."

"I was careless, I'm sorry."

It was instinctive, even then, to assume responsibility. He didn't train me to do that – he only preyed on what was already there.

There was another hesitation, his eyes drifting over my head to the space where the shore loomed in the distance, and I wiped my hair out of my face with one hand.

'You're bleeding,' his tone changed, suddenly, more curious than flat, looking at the curve of my neck, "you hit your head."

As if on cue, my pulse quickened, and I felt my kicking grow wilder in spite of myself. Phantom fish flitted against the bottoms of my feet and my breath caught in my throat.

"Let's get me out of the water, then," I said lightly, flinching at how forced I sounded even to my own ears, "before I become someone's lunch."

He blinked, and just like that he was reaching for me, grabbing my wrists and lifting me easily, sitting back as I crumpled into a puddle onto the deck.

"Let me see," he lifted my hair, his fingers coming away tinted red, "we should probably head back in. Easier to clean it off at home."

"You pushed me," I said, in spite of myself, and something like danger flickered through his eyes before he looked puzzled, one corner of his mouth twitching upward.

"Did nobody ever teach you how to swim like that?" he asked, smiling, "that's how I learned, anyway."

There was a lesson in there,
Wren

40

Sawyer,

While away at college (and therefore away from me and my clearly superior judgment) you started dating a very terrible girl.

I would like to clarify, though it should go without saying, that I do not typically bear ill will toward girls in general or even the girls you date/kind of date/see casually, though I will admit I require constant validation and sometimes feel something like resentment instead, though that has nothing to do with her specifically.

(I would absolutely love for you to date someone who can also be my best friend, so that we can be best friends without you and gossip about you on the couch when you go to the bathroom.)

Her name was Isabella, but she went by Bella, and you know I've always found that ironic since she was only pretty on the outside. I still hate her, but that's beside the point.

Despite rarely seeing her after you dropped out, you continued to date for a year, growing serious enough that I began to worry you were going to propose and spend the rest of your life with this very terrible girl who clearly hated me. You knew how I felt, but given my circumstances, you elected to make your own decisions (bad ones, but again, beside the point).

Bella liked to fill her social media stories with photos and videos that made the viewers pause, to hesitate and wonder whether they should be concerned. Your phone would light up and there she'd be with her crinkle-eyed, white-toothed grin, leaving just enough of her surroundings visible to make you squint. Videos of her acting out wildly, hysterical giggling shouts of "Bella, stop!" in the background, dissolved into "I miss you" and "when are you coming to see me" texts.

She was a stunner, both physically and in personality, the kind of person who makes you feel like the most hilarious person in the room; but she could turn off and redirect her charm at the drop of a hat. The first time I met her, she was all giggles and (sometimes backhanded) compliments and disarmingly earnest listening skills. Two hours after she left, her best friend followed me on Instagram and, when I followed back, promptly blocked me. Your reunions were fraught with drama and tears. To each their own, I know, and we don't have a leg to stand on when it comes to judging how others show affection; but you wanted commitment, and she did not.

She came home with you once for spring break, and was wholly disappointed that we weren't a coastal party city. I don't know what you saw in her, mostly because I never asked, but while she was made for someone, it wasn't you.

I won't go into details, because I'm more into talking about myself and my many issues than I am making you relive yours, but I will reiterate that I received at least 200 too many alarmingly vicious social media messages from a girl who claimed to know what you wanted better than I did.

Of course, I wasn't exactly in my prime at this point, and all arguments I had against her were easily dismissed given my own lack of initiative. But for the most part, you listened, and just ignored me afterward.

Except when it came to me, and, recently miffed by your own Cam encounter, you had no time for my double standards.

"Your entire relationship is so toxic, and you don't even *see* it," I accused, which, in retrospect, was sort of hypocritical.

"That's rich; coming from the girl who lets her boyfriend hit her."

I reeled back like I'd been slapped; saw the instantaneous regret in the drop of your shoulders and the bow of your head before you'd even turned back around to face me.

"I don't *let* him," I spit, my words far weaker than I aimed for them to be.

"Wren – "

"I don't *let him*," I swatted your hands away when you reached for me, and you pulled them back in surrender.

"I'm sorry, I didn't mean – "

"You said it," I shrugged my sweatshirt on and half-jogged down the stairs of your apartment, flinching instinctively at the sound of your feet following close behind mine.

"Wren," you reached over my head to catch the door as I pulled it open, and I yelped when it slammed back shut, recoiling and glancing off your chest. You winced, raising your hands behind your head, taking a step back, "I'm sorry, I didn't mean it. I shouldn't have said it, I just got mad – "

"You know what?" I tilted my chin up to face you, pulling the door open again and taking the first step out, "you sound a lot like him."

You don't,
Wren

41

Sawyer,

Please read this one knowing all that you do now and knowing that I would have told you if things hadn't already gone the way that they did.

Please understand, also, that I know this is not justification. I disliked her for many reasons (though I promise I tried), but I can't pretend that what happened in the future excuses the way I acted in the past.

(I'm learning too, see?)

By the time the holidays in 2010 rolled around, we were already fairly set in our ruts. You had moved back from school; I had been living at Cam's for roughly a year and we were both lying to ourselves daily about the nature of our relationships.

The day started off well enough – I was at your parents' house long before Doug and Penny, before Cam was finished with his workout. I was elbow-deep in flour and surrounded by pie crusts when you walked in the door – all good and well, since before I had time to dust myself off and tackle you, Bella appeared at your side.

"Hi Robin!" she cooed as she set a sequined duffle bag at the foot of the stairs, and you murmured *be nice* in my ear as you bent to kiss my temple (rude).

"Hi Bella," I held out my powdery palm, which she smiled at but made no move to take, "it's Wren."

She hurried toward your mom, presenting her gift with a

crinkle-nosed smile, and your dad winked at me from the opposite end of the kitchen.

"Tie on an apron, boy, these pies ain't gonna bake themselves," I hip-checked you, and you grabbed your apron and threw it over your head with a flourish. Bella took a seat across the table from you, watching as we latticed crusts and spatula-ed out fillings and sampled cinnamon-sugar crusted apples.

"You two are totally long-lost siblings," she said after awhile, in that forced way that everyone who has ever liked either of has said – as though them saying it is meant to make our proximity to each other suddenly incestuous, to send us lurching in opposite directions.

"It's hard to tell where one begins and the other ends," came the echo, tersely, from the doorway.

"Hello, Cam," your mom sang, and he flashed her one of his killer smiles, presenting her with two bottles of sparkling juice, "oh, what a doll!"

"Hello, Cam," Bella stood abruptly to introduce herself, and I caught myself before I rolled my eyes too violently, "I'm Bella."

"This is Sawyer's friend from school," your dad reached out to shake Cam's hand as well, cutting Bella short, "Bella, this is Wren's boyfriend."

"Put me to work!" Cam clapped once, grinning at me and deliberately avoiding your gaze, "need any help with the pies, babe?"

"We're actually almost done," I turned my cheek so he could kiss it, one hand cupping my hip possessively (how I had loved it – that feeling of being someone's, of being wanted so clearly and openly), "but I can join you in the living room with a cup of coffee in a minute if you want."

"Coffee's right here, Cam," your mom called, and I flinched

when I saw his eyes flash toward her, "help yourself. I assume you know how Wren takes hers?"

"I can get my own," I started, and though nobody else seemed to notice, I saw your eyes flicker toward us almost imperceptibly.

"I got it. See you in there," he gave me a squeeze – this one a little more forceful than necessary – and ducked into the kitchen.

"Everything okay?" you whispered, without looking up from your expertly-crimped crust.

"Yeah. Of course."

"Are you s-"

"Sawyer."

The front door opened at that moment, my parents spilling in carrying boxes of side dishes and earning cheers from us all for their presence alone. The first few hours were always the best – I love even your extended family, don't get me wrong – but there is something so relaxed and warmly disorganized about the time before everyone else arrives. Penny grabbed me and dramatically stamped my face with kisses as though it had been years instead of days since she'd seen me last. Doug joined your dad in their usual discussion on how best to cook the meat. Once all of the adultier adults were present, we were banished to go be social in other rooms of the house.

Bella had followed Cam into the living room, and the two were deep in discussion by the time you and I walked in.

"Oh my god Robin, he is so funny," she swatted playfully at my leg as I sat between them in what little space remained (I disagree, by the way – Cam is a lot of things, some of them good, but none of them is 'funny').

"Wren," you clarified, and with one quick arch of your eyebrow noted that Cam didn't.

(Yes, I saw that.)

There's a picture on his mantle from this day. We're sitting on the couch, me leaning into Cam and his arm looped almost fully around my waist. My knee crosses over his, and his other hand rests on my thigh in such a way that his thumb has slipped under the hem of my dress as though by accident. I know now as you did then that nothing he did was unintentional – I saw your jaw clench as your mom snapped the picture, your eyes locked on the path of his fingers. his gaze met yours as the camera lowered and he smiled, soft and crooked.

The rest of the day was, as usual, mostly just a flurry of activity and voices – everyone commenting on my hair and my figure and my gorgeous boyfriend. You winking whenever you caught my eye. Cam's hand continuously on the small of my back like a tether, or a leash. Bella's laugh, genuine and hearty and clearly catching even her by surprise (for a minute there, I saw what you saw in her). Your dad swooping in for a picture with me that I later saw sitting on his desk next to your grad pictures. Cam portioning my food for me while everyone praised him for being such a gentleman. Me catching Bella in the hallway with her head tipped back.

"His dad is sober," I told her, trying to pretend that this wasn't something you would have already told her, "there's no alcohol allowed in the house."

"That's why I'm hiding in the hallway, sweetie," she whispered back, pressing a dramatic and bitter kiss to my cheek (why is everyone always kissing me?) before dancing back down the hall.

Declining dessert, kissing Cameron under a mistletoe that someone brought out far too early, the living room growing crowded, warm, overwhelming with his fingers continuously grazing the inside of my thigh as he drew me toward him.

Slipping away to make myself useful. You catching me in the kitchen with a cold can of soda pressed to my forehead.

"Doing okay, Sparrow?"

'Yeah," my mouth moved unconsciously, words falling flat. You moved toward me, past me, started hand-washing dishes so that our elbows brushed, "she's not so bad. Bella."

"Except that she is clearly drunk," you said, without looking up, "that's sort of a bummer."

"At least she's not feeling you up under the dinner table," I watched your eyebrows dart up as you snorted, surprised.

"Oh, you think that, do you?"

We both laughed then, for real – surprising ourselves.

I almost asked you then, *why are we doing this?*, almost said it out loud, almost wanted to throw one of your t-shirts on over that uncomfortable dress and throw myself down on the couch in the basement and let the party upstairs carry on without me, let the world carry on without me. You opened your mouth to speak. Thought better of it. The moment passed, and I never said it – not just then but for as long as the charade continued.

"I've never had so many people comment on my body before. And I've lived in some rough houses, let me tell you," I cracked the can of soda open, lifted it to my lips.

"You look real good, Wren," you finally lifted your eyes to mine, "but how do you feel?"

I didn't say anything. This moment passed, too. I started towel drying beside you, placing dishes in their designated cabinets with the ease of having done it a thousand times before.

"That dress," you finally said, as the sink drained and we hung the towels up to dry, "it doesn't…. I mean. It leaves plenty to the imagination, it's gorgeous. But it doesn't leave a whole lot of room for error."

I glanced toward the doorway, half expecting Cam to appear there at the very suggestion.

"I don't have anything to hide."

"Does he?"

I grabbed the hem of my dress and lifted, exposing my tiny shorts and bare abdomen. You quickly averted your eyes in a motion almost like an eyeroll, making a pained sound in the back of your throat.

"Not a mark," I hissed, letting the fabric fall smoothly back into place as I stepped so close to you there was no chance of our voices carrying, "why can't you just let it go?"

You looked offended by the suggestion, and opened your mouth to say what I'm sure would have been something justifiably indignant – but at that moment your aunt popped her head in and chirped, "family picture!"

We were both flushed, I'm sure, but to her credit she pretended not to notice.

"Wren, why don't you go grab Cameron? He went to go see the rest of the house."

Here is where I left you. Here is what I never told you.

I saw them through the doorway in your dad's study, the light soft and amber and shadow filled. One hand slipped between the folds of his shirt, one leg fitted between hers. There was no mistaking it. I won't give them that. I will say that Bella had the decency to look embarrassed as I rapped my knuckles on the doorframe, fixing her skirt and skittering past me with what sounded like an apology.

"I'll tell him," was all I managed to get out, and she nodded once, vanishing around the corner. To Cam – clear eyed and nonchalant, the buttons of his shirt still half-undone – I said nothing.

He stood slowly, leisurely, tidying himself before me until it was almost as though I had imagined the whole scene. And I stood there, stricken, silent, until he slipped through the doorway beside me and let his lips graze my ear.

"Don't think you're any better," he whispered, and then we walked back into the living room hand-in-hand, as though nothing had happened. I realized, then, my face frozen in a fragment of a smile and my eyes glazed over, that I was familiar with the way he and Bella skirted around each other once I was in the room, with the sudden shift in the angle of his shoulders and the funny hitch in his step. I'd seen it before with his coworkers, with the women he'd introduce me to as 'old friends'. The only thing new about this was that this time he had allowed himself to be caught.

You broke up with Bella that evening, as you dropped her off at the airport so that she could make it home for Christmas.

"Don't look at me like that," you said when you told me, and I had started to speak.

I still could have told you. But I didn't.

"I'm not looking at you like anything," I said instead, and I let you move on in the way that I couldn't.

> *But that's not fair to you either, is it?*
> *Wren*

42

Love of My Life,

I never told you why.

Each time I showed up after a particularly heavy absence, hospital bracelet still snug around my wrist, shadows under my eyes, I didn't explain myself.

I couldn't tell you. I couldn't look you in the eyes and explain to you how you weren't enough to make me want to live. Nothing was. I couldn't tell you that I knew I was no longer capable of deciding for myself, that I had grown so dependent on him that he knew what was best for me more than I did myself.

But I'm not looking you in the eyes right now, and if you've made it this far then that means I probably would be able to now, anyway.

November 2009: I parked my car in Cameron's garage and read a book with the engine running. He got home about two minutes after I fell asleep. I spent two weeks in the hospital on 24-hour watch while they monitored me for permanent damage. They said I was lucky that I would make a full recovery. I didn't feel lucky.

April 2010: After pinning me to the wall face-first until my vision started spotting, I rushed back into consciousness to the sound of Cam howling as my fingers raked across his skin. When I saw his blood under my nails I knew for sure he would kill me. Instead, he comforted me. I listened wearily to him apologizing for hurting me in his attempts to save me from myself. I spent a week and a half heavily medicated in a blurry beige room.

January 2011: Cam brought in the New Year with promises and expensive whiskey. I used them both to wash down as many pills as I could find. I vaguely recall vomiting in the back of an ambulance, in the entrance to the ER, in what looked and felt like the inside of a tilt-a-whirl. Twenty-one days in a rehab facility.

August 2011: you dropped me off at the end of the block after driving me back from my brief stint in a cell. Cam was sleeping when I climbed into bed, and he didn't speak of it the next morning when I brought him his coffee. He didn't say anything about it until he dropped me off for what has so far been my final involuntary admittance. He didn't say anything of any importance in spite of my questions, my persistence, the shrill notes of my voice as it rose in panic. It wasn't until he was walking out that he leaned in, lips brushing my ear in what would have looked to anyone else like a kiss, and whispered, "this time, you'll be better."

And so I have been.

This excludes, of course, midnight ER visits and excuse-laden trips to Urgent Care, evenings and sunny afternoons spent tucked away in the bathroom, self-medicating.

It also excludes all of the times I showed up on your doorstep or in your kitchen, appropriating your icepacks or your steady hands to butterfly-tape split skin and gently test for fractures.

I've been better, Sawyer. You've made sure of it.

You always do,
Wren

43

The Great Love of My Life,

Breaking the news of our engagement to you wasn't exactly the celebratory experience one would expect it to be.

"Hey," I leaned against the front bumper of the truck you were elbow-deep in, keeping my hand tucked under my arm and my shoulders curved inward, "can I talk to you?"

"Yeah," you wiped your hands on your jeans, nodded toward your coworkers, and guided me out the back with one hand hovering near the small of my back.

"Please try to be happy for me," I said once the door had clicked shut behind us, and your eyes immediately dropped to the crook of my arm, your jaw tightening.

"Okay. Let's see it."

I extended my hand toward you, and after a pause you pulled your hand from your pocket and took my fingertips in yours, raising it upward.

"That's a serious rock you've got there, Sparrow."

I knew my smile was halfhearted at best, because you didn't meet my gaze for another few moments, and when you did your eyes were shadowed and your lips were pursed slightly, dimples pronounced.

"He's a serious guy."

You released my hand and watched it fall back to my side, my fingers curling into a loose fist.

"You said yes, Wren?"

And I kept my voice low when I answered you, because neither of us was pretending anymore.

"What do you think he would have done if I hadn't?"

Your lashes were dark on your cheeks and darker still when you lifted your eyes skyward and blinked hard, inhaling slowly through your nose.

"Do you have a plan? Have you given any thought to what we talked about?"

"I don't have the time to make a plan, Sawyer. I don't have the wherewithal to make a plan."

"I can do it. I can get you out of this. Please, just let me help you."

"This isn't about you, Sawyer. It *cannot be about you,* or there is no point at all to me fighting him on it every single day. If this is about you, then I have been lying to him all along and maybe I've deserved everything I've got."

You've always been terrible at hiding your emotions from me, particularly strong ones and particularly when they catch you off guard, as they seem to do nowadays.

"What's that supposed to mean?" your voice was quiet and forceful, your eyes darting over my head like you expected someone to be there waiting.

"If I stopped seeing you, if I stopped talking to you, if I cut you out of my life the way he wants me to, Sawyer, what else would he have to be angry about? If I'm doing this all because you want me to, then he's right and I'm sneaking around behind his back for some other guy. If it's for me – if I'm pushing him because you matter to me and this matters to me, then he's wrong and I'm not because you came first. This cannot be about you. It has to be about me."

I saw the flash in your eyes as you considered telling me yet again that it had never been about anyone but him, but you knew then and I know now that I needed to believe it to survive.

"So what? You marry him and you have his kids and you live this perfect little domesticated existence and pretend he doesn't throw you around when he gets a little drunk? Or angry? Or bored?"

"I'm not going to marry him, Sawyer."

"You also said you weren't going to stay with a guy who hit you, so I think it's safe to assume you're having a little trouble sticking to your guns, Wren."

"Thanks for the advice, I hadn't noticed how terrifyingly shitty my life had become. You're a real pal."

"Wren – "

"He knows I'm here. Did you know that? He told me it was okay if I came here to tell you that we're going to get married and also that he thinks we should see each other probably 100% less than we do."

"And you listened?"

"He's my fiancé."

"*Well maybe he shouldn't be!*" you threw your hands up into the air, laughing humorlessly, and spun on your heel, "honestly, Wren, have I not given you enough options? Do you not think that literally anything would be better than this?"

"Do you not think that I've spent time considering my options? Do you think that I would still be here if I thought that *literally anything* would be better for everyone?"

"Don't think about anyone else, Wren. Don't think about anyone else for once in your life and just go. Get out of here and don't wait to see what happens or look back or wait to see if it gets better. It's not getting better. It's never going to get any better no matter how hard you try to love him into a better version of himself because *he is not capable of loving you the way that you deserve."*

"Neither am I, Sawyer."

Neither am I,
Wren

44

Sawyer,

Would you like some more praise? Wouldn't we all?

I never woke you up when I had nightmares. All those times that you'd come to, instantly alert and reaching up to where I was sleeping on the bed or the couch or the cot near you – you did that of your own accord.

My nightmares are silent; I wake up with every muscle clenched, my teeth creaking from the sheer force of containing whatever it is that's trying to escape between them. I've never made a sound in my sleep. Even when I wake up, it's without a sound. My eyes open and my breath catches, and it takes a moment before I can exhale. And that's when you would wake up. In the moment between the waking and the breathing.

Usually, you were quiet, too. You'd link fingers with me and let our hands hang between us, a reassuring presence until I would unwind enough to speak first.

But on the really bad ones, the ones that would leave me holding on so tight that both of our knuckles were white, you'd start talking.

Where did you learn that? To just speak about nothing in particular, describing our surroundings and telling me the time and the date and the weather. And eventually, slowly, I would reenter the waking world.

Somehow, Sawyer, you always know what to do. It's like all the hesitation that burdens me bypassed you entirely and puts all the right words in your mouth and actions in your mind at exactly the right moment.

Know what one of my favorite moments of all time was? I absolutely could not tell you this to your face, because I already know you'd have that doofy grin and I'd be entirely unable to make eye contact with you in spite of our nearly flawless communication skills.

Remember when we had friends (ha) and went to holiday parties and did gift exchanges and made peppermint cookies and pretended it was cold and snowy outside?

I went mostly for you – that's no secret, just like it was no secret how grateful I am that you let me hang on you like a moth to a flame, never letting me stray more than a few feet away, your fingers always finding my belt loop or coat pocket to tug me closer. I will never be a person who feels at home in a crowd unless you're there. That probably says more about you than it does about me, but I'm okay with it either way. Because you make me feel genuinely at home no matter where we are.

But that's not my favorite moment. My favorite moment came right on the coattails of one of my least favorites, because nothing is quite as humiliating to me as undivided attention by more than one person at a time in any situation.

At this particular festivity, a mistletoe had been hung in the kitchen doorway, and countless couples or hopeful souls were unceremoniously shoved beneath it either by their supportive friends or by each other. Each new pairing was met with lighthearted whoops and whistles from the crowd. We found ourselves propelled backward until our shoulders met in the dim light and the room grew suddenly muffled as what felt like hundreds of eyes fell upon us. You clocked what I'm sure was absolute terror on my face in that brief moment where I was suddenly the center of attention, and you remedied the situation in the best way possible. With not a second of hesitation you took my face in your hands and peppered me with rapid-fire kisses from hairline to chin, catching every inch but my mouth, progressing to my ears and shoulders and the crown of my head when I (and everyone else in line of sight) burst out laughing. When you felt you'd done your part, you held my hand above our heads like I was the winner of a boxing match, and announced, "is that sufficient?" to our audience.

The tension was diffused, the mood was lifted, and there were no more attempts to coerce us into romance from that day forward.

What's different about you is that, while you always seem to know what to do and when to do it, you don't necessarily trust yourself that you've done it.

Because later that night, bumping hips with me on the way out to your car, you paused and waited for me to lift my gaze to yours. You arched your eyebrows, dipping your head and looking immensely relieved when I grinned back at you.

That tiny bit of self-doubt somehow makes all the things you do better. You're impulsive, but in a wholesome and often self-deprecating way. However sure you are about something in the moment, you always want to remedy any uncertainties as soon as possible.

And if I had refused to make eye contact, if I had run out of the room or failed to smile when you came to pick me up the next morning, you would have apologized profusely. Because you also understand that apologizing doesn't mean that you did something wrong on purpose.

You have a lot of qualities that others should consider taking note of. The world would be a much better place if we had a few more like you.

I trust your gut more than you do, Sawyer. You make me feel safe.

Always Yours,
Wren

45

Sawyer,

You weren't allowed to visit me when I was admitted, so I'll tell you what the inside of the psychiatric ward was like.

That faint, dingy light that always permeates the air in hospitals was stronger than ever. The walls, the ceiling, the floors – even the people were yellow. My hands appeared jaundiced and aged, and I'm sure my face would have as well, had I been allowed to see my reflection.

I remember thinking, the moment they shut the door to my room and left me there in the ringing silence, that I was not sick, was not meant to be here, but that I would be both of those things if I didn't get out soon.

I didn't sleep at all for the first two nights. Three times in the first 24 hours, other patients were brought in screaming, strapped down to rolling stretchers and writhing against their restraints. Twice, the shrieks were so pained, so desperate, that it took all I had not to join in. For 72 hours I was not allowed to shower, change my hospital-issued pastel blue scrubs or even my underwear, nor was I given deodorant, a toothbrush, mouthwash. By the end of day three I was ready to claw off my own skin, strip down and scrub myself clean with my bare hands using only the antibacterial soap and lukewarm water from the sink in the bathroom I was never allowed to be alone in. That night, twenty minutes before lights out, one of the neutral-faced, bleary-eyed nurses came to my room and led me to a single dimly-lit shower with floor-to-ceiling beige tile and no curtain. I was given a small (yellow) bar of soap, used, and wasn't given a towel until I was finished. The nurse stood disinterestedly in the corner the entire time, only speaking when my ten minutes was up. I was handed new scrubs, but because I had not admitted myself (not that I would have known what to pack if I had), I was given only my own dirty underwear back.

I turned it inside out and cried myself to sleep.

Because he was paying, and because I seemed to be the only one who didn't know what was going on, I was given a cocktail of medications twice daily.

On day six, after three showers and forgoing undergarments completely, I was brought a "gift" from my fiancé containing only a six pack of Hanes cotton boy-shorts, two of my own underwire-free bras, and a list of times when he would be free to answer his cell if I called.

I knew these were instructions, and so I did.

"Please come and get me, Cam," I pleaded, quietly, the phone pulled tight to me, my shoulders curved inward, "I'm sorry. I'll try harder. I'll be better. It's not good for me here."

"I'm trying to help you," he insisted, in a voice so calm and well-rehearsed that I believed it, "I just want you to be safe. You're a danger to yourself right now, sweetheart. They know what they're doing. They're only trying to make you better."

"Please. I'm sorry," I could feel the tears burning behind my eyes, ducked my head so the nurses wouldn't see and take me back to my room, "it won't happen again. You know it won't. It was a mistake. I know that now."

"I'll come visit you this weekend, okay?"

"Cam," the desperation in my voice was almost too much to

keep low, to keep between the two of us, "if I have to stay in here, I'm not going to make it."

"You need to give this time. You don't have a choice. This is for your own good."

"I don't feel any better," I was too loud, catching the attention of someone down the hall, and I turned away, ducked my head, "I feel so much worse. Cam, they wouldn't let me shower for three days. I just got the clean underwear you sent me last night. There are too many people in here who are so much worse off than I am. They don't have you to help them. There aren't enough people here to care about all of us. Please, come bring me home. I promise I'll be better."

After two weeks of the same routines, the same washed-out light, the same footsteps squeaking down the hallway to peer in on us as we pretended to sleep; I said what he wanted.

"I'm never going to get any better without you, Cam. I need you."

He discharged me the next day.

Don't think I don't see it,
Wren

46

The Great Love of My Life,

Part of the problem with being a person that people feel they can confide in is that so often you are told things you wish you hadn't been. People look at me and the words spill out of them. I'm stained dark with them on the inside.

I felt it in the hospital the day my roommate told me she got into cars with boys who drove too fast and too recklessly all while knowing what could go wrong; she left her seatbelt undone and her feet on the dashboard. She told me that she hoped for a lapse, a mistake, an error that would take her life from her so that she wouldn't have to do it herself. And then she laughed, her perfect teeth clamping down on her lower lip when she realized how casually she had let that slip.

I told you that the only way I would ever get away from him was in a body bag. Your eyes flickered the way I'm sure mine did when she told me.

Those kinds of things sit heavy in your heart. And you keep them to yourself because they aren't your truths to tell. They weigh on you, though it feels silly to drown in them because it's not even your pain that's causing it.

I shouldn't have said that to you, no matter how true it feels. It wasn't fair to make you carry that around with you for the rest of your life when I already know how it feels to do the same. I'm sorry. I have to believe I was wrong and that you'll never have to live with that running through your head while you're trying to sleep.

We've lived with enough truths of our own.

You and I have often had vastly different reactions to things, even with my years of learning how to smother myself. You are calm and reserved and composed, I am fiery and loud and explosive. We see things differently. Our memories of the same events are vastly different but usually just as great.

Or just as awful.

It was a Thursday when I found out, of course, and I came to you as I always do.

I came to you hollow and vacant as I had ever been, trying valiantly to keep my face blank in spite of the whirlwind going on inside my head. I don't have to keep my face blank with you – that was the panic working, the instinct.

You looked up from under the hood and I saw the gears turning, but instead of coming to me you let me take a seat on the workbench and chew on my thumbnail while you finished. When you approached, wiping your hands on the rag tucked into the pocket of your jeans, I looked up, my features unnaturally composed, my eyes bright and empty.

"What's going on, Sparrow?" you asked, softly, purposefully. You kept your voice low enough to not draw the attention of any of the guys, who had already greeted me and gone back to work.

"I think I have a problem," I replied, and you grabbed your keys off the barstool nearest to you and helped me onto the floor, guiding me out the back door and across the gravel lot to the field out back.

It was a cooler day than usual for May, the breeze making the hair on the back of my neck and arms rise up and chill me. You guided me down the path by my elbow until we'd reached the treehouse your dad made you when you were still small enough to fit inside it.

"What do we do?" you asked.

Sawyer, you were so ready. You were ready before you even knew what you were going into. I have full confidence that if I had told you in that moment that I'd killed someone (but specifically Cam) and needed help hiding the body, you'd have still been on board without hesitation.

(Was that not funny? I thought it was funny.)

But there was no way for you to be ready for what I told you. You did the best you could to be as stable as you could. You apologized later. But this is how I saw it.

"My period is late," I told you, and all at once the entire world stopped turning around us.

"Okay."

"I'm sure, Sawyer."

"Okay."

"He can't know."

"No."

"I have to go now."

You nodded, and we stood there in silence for a lifetime, a quiet that was so unprecedented from you that it actually relieved me to know how hard you were thinking me through this.

"Okay. Okay. I'll talk to my dad; I'll tell him I need to take a break for awhile. He won't ask questions. We'll figure it out. It's okay."

"You don't have to come with me."

The look on your face – like it had never occurred to you that we didn't have to be in this together.

'We can leave tonight. Or by tomorrow morning, if there's anything you don't want to leave behind."

"Sawyer. I can't ask you to come with me."

"I know," you said, your voice level as you worked your way through a thought, "you don't have to."

The weight of it pressed down on me until I thought I'd never be able to speak again, but I did.

"I need a few days."

You didn't contact me. You knew better.

But you were ready nonetheless, when I came to you four days later with anxious energy burning off of me and my skin nearly bursting to contain it.

"Are you ready? Where are your things?" you stood up straight, setting your tools down, your eyes flickering over me like you were trying to account for the presence of all of my limbs.

"It's okay," I told you, though that wasn't at all what I meant, and I just couldn't find the right words.

"Okay. We can go now. Let me just tell my dad – "

"No, Sawyer," I reached out and grabbed your arm, and you went still at my touch like I'd frozen you solid, "it's okay."

You took my elbow and guided me through the shop and out to your car, opening the passenger door and waiting for me to duck in before closing it firmly behind me. You took your time walking around the back, dragging your feet and running your hand through your hair.

"We can still go, you know," you said once you'd sat down, staring somewhere past the windshield into the trees, "there's still no reason to stay."

"There's always been reasons to stay, Sawyer," I whispered, trying so hard not to cry because I knew you were, too, "it's just that for a minute there I thought I might have had a more important reason to leave."

You didn't say anything for a long time, and then you put the car in drive and just started going, nowhere we had ever been, me staring out the window and you pretending that you weren't glancing over at me every few seconds to make sure I was still remembering to breathe.

You pulled off onto a two-rut road that curved back into the woods, making a wide arch until we came to a small garage in a clearing it hardly fit into. You parked and got out of the car, sifting through the pile of rocks along the tree line until you picked up a key, then nodded toward the door so I got out and followed you.

There was no overhead light, only one single window leaking dusty air over the room. Stacked against one wall was a tower of storage bins, a dirty wooden workbench containing several less dirty tools, and a shovel.

The light filtering through the open door behind us lit up an unassuming silver vehicle, two backpacks and a stack of blankets in the back seat.

"It's a 1998. A little on the old side, but she still runs," you kept your voice level, casual, "if someone stops by now and then, makes sure everything starts up and gets some use, you'd be able to get a few more years of driving in, easily."

"Sawyer."

"There's cash in a lockbox under the driver's seat. The code is my birthday. The backpacks have some basics – sweatshirts, socks, underwear, a couple wardrobe staples in there too."

"Sawyer."

"The tank is full. The tabs are updated. It's not insured, so you'll have to drive carefully. Just don't get in any accidents and you'll be fine."

I think I threw my arms around you a little too hard, because you staggered backward before you pulled me closer, in one of those hugs where I can feel you trying not to crush me while still holding me as tightly as possible.

"I'm not leaving," I murmured into your sleeve, and you faltered a little, "I don't have to."

"Wren," you clenched your fist in my hair, "you still can. You can do this."

"I'm not ready."

"You're never going to be ready. There's never going to be a perfect time for you to leave. But you have to. You have to go."

"You're the last person anyone saw me with. Do you think he won't ask questions?"

"You're an adult. You can go wherever you want. You can leave whenever you want."

"It's not that simple anymore, Sawyer."

Your voice got louder, less composed, and you let go of me to rub your fingers against your temples like I was giving you the world's worst and most instantaneous headache.

"Why not?"

"You know *why not*. Sawyer, if I'm not ready when I do this, he *will* find me. Do you think if it's hard for him he'll just stop? He's not keeping me around because it's a fun little game of cat and mouse. This is so far beyond anything that you think it is."

"There's no way for him to follow you. It's all cash, there's no record of you being here, there are no ties to you – "

"He started the fire."

Every time I caught you off guard it was another blow to me, how bad things really had to be for you to look at me like that.

"How do you know?"

"The same way I know he's the one who drugged me so that he could play Knight in Shining Armor."

"You didn't tell anyone? You didn't tell me?"

"There's no evidence. Believe me, he made sure of it."

"How could you know that without filing a report? How could you know – "

"I don't know if you remember how many times I've been admitted, Sawyer, but I do."

You swallowed, and I watched your fingers curl and uncurl against your thigh as you thought.

"Okay," you said, and walked back out to your car, feet crunching on the gravel as you went.

Thank you,
　　　Wren

47

The Amazing Sawyer Moore,

    I had a key to your house from the moment you moved out. It wasn't a question, or an offering; you slipped it onto my key ring one day while we were together, and I started using it to let myself in while I waited for you to get home from work.

    There were six keys on my key ring, and Cam kept track. He noticed at some point, probably early on, that he didn't know whose house the fifth key unlocked. He didn't tell me. I didn't know. I would have warned you.

    I noticed that it was gone, but he was with me. I couldn't text you to ask if you'd taken it, and for obvious reasons I couldn't ask him if he'd seen it. We were sitting on the front porch, him working on his third beer, me nursing the same cup of tea I'd come out with. It was quiet, but silences with Cam had long since stopped being comfortable ones. You didn't ruin a good day; you didn't ruin a moment of safety for me. I know you've wondered, and I've told you, but it's the truth. Cam was always unpredictable, and nothing you said or did made any difference in the long run.

    I heard your car door slam, but I was so deep into my book that I didn't realize it was you until Cam scoffed softly, and I looked up. You were moving faster and more deliberately than I had ever seen you move before, and the piece of paper clenched in your fist fluttered pathetically to the wood paneling in front of me when you whipped it at him, eyes wild.

"Is this supposed to be some sort of threat?" you asked, and I found myself sinking backward at the venom in your voice even while I reached for the note.

Nice place, was all it said, in Cam's handwriting.

"I just thought I'd let you know while I was returning your key. I'm going to have to ask you to calm down," his voice was level, a sharp contrast to the anger radiating off of you.

"That key didn't belong to you. It belongs to her. I didn't give you permission to come into my house – "

"And I didn't give you permission to harass the two of us on my front porch, and yet here you are."

"You're a real piece of work, you know that?" you jabbed your finger at him, and I saw a thin crack in his veneer.

"Sawyer," I said, softly, and your eyes darted to mine briefly before turning back to him.

"Sawyer," Cam mocked in a quiet falsetto, "you might want to listen to her. She seems a little frightened of you."

You have never been violent. Even your anger manifests as nervous energy, your emotions always tilting toward empathy.

Which is why this rage was so much more terrifying, both to Cam and to me.

You grabbed him by the front of his shirt, wrenching him to his feet so that the glass bottle fell from his hand and rolled across the ground, foam spilling out the top and trailing behind it. I stood, too, but took a step backward toward the railing.

"*Wren* has no reason to be afraid of me," you growled, and I saw the sharp flash of genuine fear in his eyes before he regained some of his composure.

"What are you going to do to me, Sawyer? Do you honestly think she'd lie for you if you hurt me?"

I'm sorry. I'm so sorry.

Your fist snapped off three teeth and sent blood bubbling out of his mouth almost immediately. He reeled and stumbled against the doorframe, his eyes wide and the closest to regretful I had ever seen. And then he lunged, toppling the two of you over the porch railing next to me and raining blow after blow upon you, most of which you shielded. You each got a few good swings in, and I stood backed into the corner breathing heavily and trying to quiet the roaring in my ears.

He broke your nose, which I knew from the sound it made and the way my own ached in response. Unsurprisingly, though, he caused far less damage to you than he ever did to me. You cost him nearly three grand in dental bills, which he refused to stick you with either out of pride or maybe just so that he would have something to hold over me later.

By the time the police came tearing up the street, the dispatcher still talking to me while I narrated frantically to her (I'm sorry, but I really thought he was going to kill you), you were both spitting blood and throwing weaker punches, still fueled by your hatred for each other but losing the strength to drive it.

I stumbled down the lawn toward you as the cops climbed from their vehicles, hands resting on their holsters, shouting, throwing my hands up and putting myself between you and them like a sacrifice.

You stopped immediately, falling backward onto your heels and then nearly onto your side, blood streaming from your nose and mouth, eyes already swelling shut.

"He broke into my house," you burbled, weakly, as they tugged your arms behind you and slapped metal links over your wrists.

"You gave us a goddamn key," Cam spit, "you're pathetic."

Your eyes flicked to mine, bloodshot and bruised, searching for something in my face that I wasn't sure how to portray.

I'm sorry, I'm sorry, I'm sorry.

Love, Wren

48

Sawyer,

    I didn't press charges.

    I saw the betrayal in your eyes as you were released, as Cam threw his arm around my shoulders and held me a little too tightly, as we went our separate ways.

    My arrival at the garage two weeks later wasn't met with the usual shouts and joking whistles, just uncomfortable shuffling eyes that flickered to the floor after meeting mine. I wove through the room, head bowed, until I reached the back and found your legs jutting out from below a rusty Civic. You recognized my feet; I could tell by the way you went still for a moment before resuming, making no move to come out and face me.

    After a few minutes of standing there under the weight of your rejection (which I entirely deserved), the length of which allowed all of your nearby coworkers to disperse awkwardly (though, even then, not without brief head-jerks of acknowledgement, which made my heart tug even harder), I knelt down and grabbed your ankles, pulling you from beneath the vehicle with relative ease with the help of your creeper.

    You stared at me, your eyes still shadowed, and then wheeled back under without a word.

    This time I dropped to my knees, fitting them between your legs, and rolled you out by your calves until you could no longer reach the car to pull yourself back.

You sat up, but I could tell it had more to do with having me hovering over you than it was actually wanting to talk, and suddenly we were inches apart, you looking down the still swollen bridge of your nose at me with your jaw jutting out.

"Does any part of you actually believe that I had a choice?" I asked, and you clenched your teeth so hard you flashed your dimples, eyes rolling upward in a clear attempt not to tear up, "because if you do, *then* you can actually not talk to me ever again."

It wasn't fair, I'm sorry. It's never been fair, the way my desperation bubbles up and over and I let it take everyone out with me.

You stood up, making sure to swing your legs clear of my face and left me kneeling there as you stalked out the back door, but you paused and glanced over your shoulder at me before it closed, so I heaved myself to my feet and followed you, getting encouraging half-smiles from the guys who were huddled around the work bench and doing their best to avoid overhearing.

I followed you to the edge of the field and down the unevenly worn path to the treehouse that was twelve years too small, keeping a fair distance between us when all I really wanted to do was chase you down and hold on.

You forgave me before the words came out; I've known you long enough to know your eyes. But it didn't stop me, didn't stop me from burying my face in my hands and pleading in a voice I didn't recognize.

"What am I going to do, Sawyer? What am I supposed to do?"

You didn't hesitate, or falter, or rightly point out the fact that I had plenty of options. Instead, you closed the gap between us and held me to your chest, your chin resting on the top of my head and my arms wrapped around yours.

    "We'll figure it out, Sparrow."

We will, won't we?
Wren

49

My One and Only,

On October 25th, Cameron went out of town for a conference lasting four days.

Taking nothing with me but the contents of my purse in the event that his conference was a ruse and I was being set up, I drove my car to the garage, and parked it in the usual spot.

I entered through the front door as I usually would if making an appointment, the little bell overhead chiming my arrival to your father. Even he was part of the plan, though we did our best to make sure that he never knew that.

"Hello, Wren," he came all the way around the counter to give me a hug, ruffling my hair as he held me at arm's length like it had been years instead of weeks since he'd last seen me up close. He always seemed to know to keep his distance when the two of us were together, like there was only so much time and he wanted to make sure there were no interruptions.

"Hi, Terry," I said, smiling under his watch no matter how I felt because your dad has always had that effect on me, "is Sawyer in?"

This was a ritual between the two of us – a habit made over years of me coming to visit you at work. He'd stroke his chin like he wasn't quite sure even though we both knew you were, and then he'd gesture toward the door to the shop and say, "why don't you go take a look?"

The guys whistled and shouted lightheartedly as I made my way in, my sweater pulled down over the palms of my hands, my scarf wound in meticulous loops around my neck. I rolled my eyes, as I always did, and they laughed and made space for me on the workbench.

Ty knelt to tug open my drawer in the tool chest, pulling out the old metal Folgers can and popping off the lid. I listened to the muffled plunk of coins landing on bills as your – our – friends swept their change in, passing it around the makeshift table.

How many hundreds of dollars do you think they've contributed over the years? I doubt I can ever pay them back for months and weeks of leftover coins, crumpled bills and the occasional wad of what they jokingly referred to as "tips" for my company.

I haven't counted it, not recently, but it's got to be nearing enough to get me out.

Every time they bring it out, I remember the satisfied look on your face the day you gave it to me. I'd already started stuffing away what I could in that bottom drawer – crumpled bills getting lost under receipts and birthday presents from people who weren't Cam.

"Here," you set it on the table in front of me with a satisfying hollow thunk, patting the top like a drum, Ty watching with hesitant glee from across the trunk of a Ford, "Wren's escape fund."

"Sawyer –" you didn't wait to let me protest before you pulled a twenty from your wallet and dropped it in, kissing me roughly on top of my head.

"Today, you're gonna learn how to change your oil."

You got it, even then; my need to do this on my own, to not be indebted to anyone, even if it was you.

I am so grateful for you each and every day.

After lunch, your dad pretended not to watch us slip out the back door and take off in your car. We had three and a half days to fill, and intentions to use every second.

We went to Disney World, leaving my phone on the coffee table at his house, taking pictures on alarmingly expensive disposable cameras and spending far more time at Epcot than we did in the actual park. You paid my way through without asking me or making eye contact so that I wouldn't have any time to do it myself.

On day two, we went to the beach – making sure to coat me with so much sunscreen that there was no possible way I could get even a fraction of a glow, much less an actual tan. I spent most of the day in the shade, anyway, building sandcastles and watching you splash around in the shallows like the huge nerd you are. You got me in the water eventually, though I spent most of the time frantically watching my feet for any sign of life, certain that I would be stung by a jellyfish or eaten by a shark if I didn't remain vigilant.

I fell asleep in your car on the way home and woke up on your futon with one of your sweatshirts zipped up over me.

By day three, I was already beginning to grow anxious at his return the next evening. I'd promised to be there when he got home from the airport, and I checked my phone continuously for flight times in case anything changed. I didn't want to go too far, in case he called to let me know he was on his way. We drove down to Ochlockonee and hiked far enough off the road to avoid being stumbled upon by swimmers or fishermen.

"Just stay," you told me, sounding more desperate than you usually did. Maybe it was that this was the most time we had spent together in over a year. Maybe it was something about the way I couldn't keep my phone out of my line of sight for more than a second or two at a time. You didn't usually fight me on him, Sawyer. You'd grown resigned to not pushing unless I did first; I did an excellent job of making you afraid to challenge me.

"I can't. He'll be home tomorrow," I didn't make eye contact, didn't let myself see the look on your face, "I promised him I'd be there."

"Why? Why, Wren? He's going to get home and then what? If he's in a good mood, you'll do what he wants, and if he isn't, he'll do what he wants anyway?"

"Sawyer," I didn't sound as angry as I wanted to. Something in my voice shook in response to your frankness.

"What? Am I wrong?"

My silence was enough of an answer.

"Come on, Wren. You can't just... you can't pretend that this is anything like it used to be. Like this is normal. Do you think this is normal?"

"He loves me. He's just jealous, Sawyer. It's not – "

"I'm jealous," you leaned in, and I stopped talking, held my breath, "I'm jealous, Wren, of all the time he gets to spend with you that used to be mine, too, but I don't *beat you because of it.*"

"He doesn't beat me. It's not like that."

"What would you call it, then? What would you call this?" you pushed up one of my sleeves, but looked instantaneously regretful when I yanked my arm back to cover up the purple handprint wrapped around my wrist, "Wren."

"He doesn't mean to," I said, and I still hate how pathetic I sounded, how desperate, making excuses for him, "he loves me."

"He doesn't," you'd never said it, not quite like that, not so outright. I'd heard 'that's not love' and 'is that what you think', but never before had you so bluntly said it, so clearly, "he doesn't love you, Wren."

"Yes he does, he loves me," I started crying for real, then, and your already defeated expression seemed to cave in on itself and grow even heavier, "he loves me, he has to love me."

We drove back to your house in silence, both of us trying to get the other to speak without saying anything ourselves. I sat with my legs pulled up to my chest, cheek resting on my knee as I stared out the window in front of me. You turned up the heat until I started to unfurl. After a few more minutes, I untied my scarf, revealing a trail of quarter-sized bruises from my chin to my collarbone. You clenched your jaw and turned away, and I swear I saw you blinking back tears. I thought it would show you – he loved me; he didn't mean to hurt me; he didn't mean to scare me.

But you saw it for what it was, a mark of his territory, his ownership, his possessiveness. I'm sure he knew, or at least assumed, that I would see you in his absence, and so he made sure you'd see that he'd staked his claim on me.

That night we fought – you not understanding why I would stay with someone who was so clearly tearing me apart, me not able to grasp that you thought leaving was even an option.

We yelled: you loudly, me frantically, and I saw you break the moment before you turned away.

I would lose you forever if I let you walk out that door; I was sure of it. And Sawyer, my heart could never take that.

Your hand was already on the doorknob when my arms encircled you, my hands gripping tight to fistfuls of your black t-shirt. The handle started turning in your hands and I pressed my lips firmly to the space between your shoulder blades, pulling you back weakly but with all the determination I had left in me.

Never in my life have I felt you so still.

You just *stood* there, Sawyer, motionless, while I desperately stamped kisses on your spine, clinging to you like the last life preserver while I pleaded incoherently through my tears, begging you to stay.

Somewhere around the fourth or fifth "I need you I need you I need you," you turned, gracefully, easily, as though we'd done this a hundred times before, drawing me against your chest and lowering your face to the curve of my neck. Your breath was hot and uneven as your mouth almost ghosted along my skin, your cheeks damp.

"Okay," you said, fitting one leg against my knees so that when you slid down to the floor I stayed with you, your shirt still bunched tight in my hands, my breath still hitching and panic-drenched, "okay, I'll stay, I'll stay."

We stayed like that – my legs hooked over yours, your face buried in the hollow of my shoulder, until your breathing stopped being quite so ragged and we stopped asking each other to make promises that we couldn't. My fingers snared in the short hairs at the nape of your neck, I whispered that I loved you, and you made a sound almost like a sob.

I could have/should have/would have been in love with you. More so in that moment than ever before, with my forehead against your temple and your kisses peppering my shoulder. And I could have stayed like that forever; I'm sure you could have, too.

But when the sun started to rise, I had no choice. You have to understand, Sawyer, that I truly believed that.

I said I was sorry and you just shook your head. *Don't be*, you were telling me, or maybe *it doesn't matter*.

Neither of us had slept, and we looked it; puffy red eyes and pale, washed-out skin gave us away. While you splashed your face with cold water in the bathroom, I set your coffee to brew and put away my makeshift bed on your couch. When I looked up from folding the last blanket, you were waiting in the doorway, eyes closed, slumped against the frame.

"I love you," I said, again, and you half-murmured, half-mouthed it back, "but I have to love him, too. I have to go home."

"I'm always here, Sparrow," you said, your voice deep and rough and raw, "you know that."

You seemed heavier, like the night had weighed you down on the inside, and I didn't have to stretch quite so much to kiss your forehead. I cupped your chin in my hand for a moment, but didn't make you look at me for too long.

I grabbed my purse, and you moved for your keys. You'd already grabbed them from the dish on the coffee table when I reached out, stopping you.

"It's only a block to the shop. I'll walk."

I left you sitting on your couch, head resting in your hands.

Cam was in a good mood when he got home. He thought it was sweet that I'd fallen asleep waiting for him.

Love, Wren

50

Sawyer Moore,

    In June of 2012, Cam and I were in a car accident.

    I broke my right arm and my nose, fractured three ribs, sustained a concussion, and needed 46 stitches over 5 areas of my body. I was heavily bruised, and dazed, and stumbled through the questions of the paramedics, flinching away from the lights they shone in my eyes.

    Cam had two broken ribs and whiplash.

    I remember seeing you, blurry and frantic, shoving past nurses and barreling toward my room with your hair still dripping from your shower and your shirt clinging to your damp skin. He stopped you with one hand, jutting out and pressing his palm hard into the center of your chest. I don't know how much time had passed; only that I was in my own glass-walled room of the ER and that the number of doctors surrounding me had significantly decreased. In my heavily disoriented state, I lurched upright in my cot, extending my arm in a gesture parallel but far weaker than Cam's, reaching for you, calling your name through lips that didn't quite keep up with my thoughts. You turned, your eyes locking with mine briefly before taking in my surroundings, darting back to Cam and the coldness of his stance.

    You knew right away.

    Two hours before the accident, Cam came home from work.

    I could feel it in the sharpness of his keys against the lock, the heaviness of his anger preceding him.

I kept my shoulders lowered, my back turned to him, scrubbing circles on the dishes in the sink while every inch of my body was attuned to his, calculating, adjusting.

"How was your day?" I asked, though I knew, because either way I was damned, and my best bet was to try and soften it.

He didn't answer, setting his keys in the dish on the cabinet and methodically rolling up the sleeves on his button-down shirt. I set the dish in the rack and dried my hands on the towel hanging by my hips, steadying myself as I turned to face him.

"Cam? Is everything okay?" I hadn't even finished speaking before he swept his hand across the table, napkins and spices and placemats flying, clattering against the walls and the floor. I jumped, my nails cutting into the palms of my hands.

"Are you just going to stand there?" his voice was level, but mocking, the corner of his mouth lifting in a sneer.

"Do you want coffee? A drink? I – "

"Do you want to tell me where you were on Wednesday night?"

I faltered, trying to think back, but he had already decided.

"If I call your boyfriend, will he hesitate before he gives me an alibi, too? Or is he a better liar than you?"

"I was at work."

"Right, because I'm supposed to trust the gossipy bitches you work with," he laughed, a sharp and unwelcome sound.

"I only stayed two hours late. I promised I'd help Ann – "

"Don't lie to me!" he slammed his fist on the table, and I knew better than to keep telling the truth or even to keep speaking at all, "and clean up this mess."

I waited until he had turned toward the stairs before I

stepped forward, kneeling to scoop salt and pepper and tabasco into my hands.

    I wasn't fast enough. I wasn't quiet enough. I felt his foot connect with my ribcage all the way into my teeth as they closed down on my tongue. My head slammed against the glass paneling of the dish cabinet, shattering the pane and instantly drawing a white-hot streak of blood from my temple. One hand splayed out before me on the floor. When my fingers connected with the broken fragments, I pitched back onto my heels, reaching out toward him in either a plea for help or to ward him off, my eyes rolling in their sockets as blood pooled in my mouth.

    "Cam – "

    "How could you do this to me? Was he the father? Did you have to tell him you lost his child?"

    Up until this moment I thought I had done so well, thought I had kept him from finding out I'd ever suspected. I should have known better. I was always a half-step behind him.

    "Cameron. No, no, I wasn't -"

    "You didn't tell me. You lied to me."

    "There wasn't anything to tell you, I didn't say anything because -"

    "You think this is *my* fault?"

    This was the moment when I realized how completely he had immersed himself in manipulating me, how intentional every move he made was. This was what it took for me to see what you had seen all along: he knew exactly what he was doing.

    He was about to say something else, but at that moment a sizeable drop of blood spilled from the corner of my lip and splashed over my hand, speckling the wood floor. His eyes followed it.

    Something in him shifted like a slide projector, and

suddenly he was reaching for me, his brow creased with concern, his lips parting as though he was about to speak. I recoiled, smearing the back of my hand against my mouth.

"Wren," he sounded genuinely concerned, and I hesitated. He took one cautious step forward, glass crunching under his shoes. Slowly, deliberately, he reached out, lifting my chin with two fingers and leaning in. When his thumb brushed the cut on my temple, I sucked air through my teeth and jerked my head back sharply, instinctively.

"Let me look," he snapped, grabbing my jaw and yanking my face toward him, pressing against the wound so that it dripped, then releasing me with an equal amount of force, "it's not that bad."

He watched as I stood, cautiously, my arm pinned to my throbbing side, keeping my body turned toward him like we were facing off for battle. He didn't move or speak as I inched toward him, past him, up the stairs. I could feel my heart in my ribs, my pulse in my teeth.

Somehow, I missed the receipt crumpled in the bottom of my purse. I forgot to leave it at the garage, forgot to throw it away, forgot to flush or burn or bury it. I forgot to turn toward him when I heard his footsteps heavy and fast on the stairs, didn't get away from the edge of the marble countertop fast enough. The ball of paper pinged off of my cheek as he burst through the bathroom doorway. One sideswipe sent my already weak legs toppling, my face connecting with the stone as I fell. I heard my nose break before I felt it, sparks fluttering behind my eyelids.

I remember him waiting a moment before kneeling down, shaking me. I remember him yanking me to my feet like a rag doll, my knees knocking against the doorframe as he pulled my arm over his shoulder. He left me near the front door, clattering around in the kitchen while I lolled my head from side to side and tried to blink some clarity back to my vision.

He chose his least favorite of the two cars. He buckled me in. He slid my sunglasses over my half-closed eyes and angled my face away from the window.

"Cameron," I bubbled through a mouthful of blood, and he ignored me as he backed out of the garage expertly, glancing up and down the street before pulling forward, "Cam."

We drove for long enough that I started to zone out, the road humming beneath us and the steady thrumming in my head growing stronger. This was it; I was sure of it, we would drive until he found somewhere nobody would think to look for me. His hand left the wheel and found the clasp of my seatbelt, undoing it with an almost absentminded flick of his wrist.

"It's such a gorgeous day," he said, turning to make sure my gaze shifted toward him, my eyes were convincingly clear enough, "we were on our way to have a picnic."

And then he spun the wheel.

He's not scared,
Wren

51

Sawyer Moore,

  I woke up in the hospital when they transferred my gurney, jostling me. The pain was steady but muted, like the day after a particularly brutal workout. I opened my mouth to speak and was greeted by the familiar taste of copper between my teeth. Cam's voice was a rumble under the cacophony surrounding me, my eyes swiveling wildly from face to face in a manic attempt to orient myself.

  "Hi there, Wren, you've been in an accident," a doe-eyed nurse leaned over to make eye contact with me, blocking out the light and drawing my focus upward, "I just need you to try and stay awake for me, alright?"

  "Cam," I burbled, though the inside of my head was ringing and I couldn't quite put my finger on why he was significant.

  "He's right here. He's fine. We just have to get you checked out, okay?"

  "Cam," I repeated, my fingers grasping weakly at the arm of the woman nearest me.

  "Hi Wren," she covered my hand with hers and hovered over me, "I'm Doctor Roth, I'm Cam's boss. He's okay, and you're going to be too, okay?"

  I wrenched my head free of the unfastened supports despite their protests, the world dipping violently until my gaze met Cam's over the chaotic space between us.

He shook his head, just once, almost imperceptibly, and I was firmly guided down onto my back again.

Hospital visits were routine for me. A visit to Cam's hospital was harder. I learned early that my job wasn't just to defend him. It was to avoid ever having to. Shifting blame and making excuses on the fly are both significantly harder to do when you're struggling to maintain consciousness.

Except for the part where *nobody asked*.

I realize now, though I was far too disoriented to notice it then, that the differences in our injuries were apparent. Shockingly apparent. But would you have seen it this time if you weren't already suspicious of his every move?

They didn't want to see, Sawyer. You try not to ask, but you've always wondered why I've stayed, why I haven't told anyone, why I've kept quiet.

I didn't.

He was out of the hospital that evening. Back at work the next day. Against his recommendation, I was kept for 48 hours of observation due to sluggish responses and uneven pupil dilation.

When I woke up the second morning, I made my way downstairs alone. I was careful to take the long way, avoiding the elevator that stopped on his floor, avoiding any doctors that may encounter him and innocently mention seeing me in the halls. I paused at corners to gauge my surroundings.

My arm in a baby-blue sling, my feet sluggish and uncompliant, I shuffled into the office of Dr Roth and gingerly took a seat when she looked up in surprise.

"He did this to me," I told her, once the silence felt ready for it.

"He was driving, yes," her voice was sympathetic, her head

tilting toward me and her brow furrowing, "he feels terrible."

"No," I swallowed, the words catching on the back of my tongue, "he did this to me."

There was a quiet that started warm and ended frigid, the temperature dropping with each passing second.

"What are you telling me, Wren?"

She didn't sound at all like she had upstairs, when she'd checked my vitals and talked me through my confusion. She sounded cautionary, defensive.

"Cam is a good driver."

If it weren't for the slight creasing between her eyes, I'd have thought she turned to stone before me.

"Cam's a good driver. He did this. He did this on purpose."

"Why would he do that?"

"To hide it. To hide me. He went too far. He went too far and he was scared – "

"I need you to stop talking for a minute – "

"He needed more help than he thought he would and he – "

"Wren, you need to *stop talking right now.*"

I stopped, exhaling, pressing my lips into a tight line.

"Do you understand what you're telling me?"

I opened my mouth to speak, but she shook her head.

"Yes or no. Do you understand what you're about to tell me?"

I nodded, once, slowly.

"Do you understand that your fiancé is one of the most gifted pediatric surgeons this hospital has ever seen? Do you realize that he has taken an oath to do no harm, that he has saved the lives of more children than either of us could ever – "

"Not me," I blurted, my arm curving around my abdomen

involuntarily, "he doesn't *do no harm* to me."

"If you keep telling me what you're telling me, I will be required to report it. I need you to understand that, Wren."

I didn't speak, just stared, a small spark of panic igniting in the pit of my stomach.

"Do you understand that?"

Again, I nodded, less firmly this time.

"If you tell me, I will need to report it, and while he is under investigation for such allegations, he will no longer be able to provide the life-saving care he has been for the children that come to this hospital. I need you to think about this for a moment, Wren, because you haven't told me anything that I couldn't have misunderstood. Are you absolutely sure that you want to report this?"

I felt myself sinking into my seat, my insides tilting with each inhale.

"If this is something you're able to work out between yourselves, please do," she spoke softly, reassuringly, her tone returning to the one she'd used with me hours before, "if this is something you can fix, I urge you to consider it."

We sat there in silence, her palms pressed flat to the desk between us, her eyes boring into mine and her shoulders set. The fire grew, expanding until it filled my lungs, my throat, my limbs.

"Just think about it," she repeated, and so I got up and left.

Love, Wren

52

Sawyer,

    I went to the police, and they sent me to Ed.

    Sitting across from him, my eyes drawn repeatedly to the picture on the shelf of him with his badge gleaming and his arm thrown around his son's shoulders, dazzling grins on both their faces – I found myself doubting Cam's story for the first time. I'd never seen him like this: polished and poised and clean-shaven, not a hint of whiskey on his breath. It was disarming, the way he carried himself like he'd never been anything but stone-cold sober.

    "I don't know how to tell you this," I fidgeted with the ring on my pinky, crossed and uncrossed my legs at the ankle. He leaned forward, resting his wrists on the edge of his desk, and nodded for me to continue, "it's about Cam."

    "Is he alright?"

    "He's… he's fine. It's not that. Sir, Cam… he's getting a little…"

    "He's shaking you up a bit."

    We stared at each other over the dark wood, his eyes cool and unyielding in spite of my attempt to pull any sort of reaction from him.

    "Yes."

    "He'll do that."

    "It's just that I – "

    "I trust that you understand why I'm not all that impressed

with you coming in here with a domestic problem."

There was a sudden ringing in my ears, and I blinked once, unsure.

"I'm sorry?"

"Do I come to your house and ask for your advice on how best to take care of the drunk tank overflow?"

I didn't respond, not quite believing what I was hearing and not at all knowing how to react.

"Whatever issues you have with my son will be resolved between you and my son. I'm not his babysitter, and I'm certainly not yours. If that's all, you can go."

"He – "

"Goodbye, Miss Jones," he stood, rapping his knuckles on his desk and then exiting the room before I had time to gather myself.

I tried, Sawyer. I tried.

I thought I tried,
Wren

53

Sawyer,

Sometimes when he's at work and I'm not, I pull out my headphones and pull up the playlist titled "Summer 2007" and let myself fall backward.

It was the summer we spent wandering the most – once you'd had your license a little longer and I'd finally got mine – and you'd gather up the songs that you only ever hear on the radio at two am, or the ones that always sound like they're being filtered through the walls of an old house. Music that tasted the way the days felt; warm and windy and salty and fleeting.

So I sit against the side of the house where the wind hits the corner and I close my eyes and I pretend that the sun is setting and the trees are singing and we're still so alive.

You are going to make some girl so full and vibrant. Someone who can match your warmth and intensity, who doesn't burst into tears at things like family dinners and watching the sunrise.

Someday you'll make her playlists and you'll go exploring and watch the sun make its way across the whole sky.

Cam promised me adventure, promised me skylines and souvenirs and memories. He promised me a lot of things that he chose not to deliver. Things were always my fault, one way or another.

At first, Sawyer…

At first, I caught a glimpse of it. We would hike to waterfalls high enough for sprawling views of Spanish-moss smothered trees. I would climb the railings and stretch myself over the edges, and he'd hook one finger through my belt loop and tug me toward him, ready to keep going before I had even caught my breath. He was always moving, always veering in another direction while I followed him in an awestruck stupor.

"We can keep doing this," he assured me, parked on some side road with his hand on my thigh while I circled destinations on crisp new maps and planned adventures, "we can go wherever you want."

But we didn't. He was working, or busy, or I failed to meet some end of a deal I couldn't ever remember making. Soon my eager anticipation wore down to hesitation and finally nothing at all. And then, once I'd been worn down enough, once I was tired enough – then he would reward me with gifts and affection and the intoxicating personality I had fallen in love with in the first place. I started shrinking inward, trying to make myself worthy of his warmth.

And sometimes I was, and it was glorious.

He took me out on the boat – something I'd never done before and that terrified me almost as much as it excited me. I stayed mostly to the center of the deck, one arm hooked around the railing that led below deck, despite the slow roll of the water and the fact that he rarely even wore a life vest. It wasn't scary then, not truly – though now the idea of being alone on the open water with him makes my blood run cold – but it was a good kind of frightening. The world dipping and rising beneath us for miles, seagulls screeching overhead and the wind carrying us where it pleased.

"When did you have time to get so sunkissed?" you mused, one evening over dinner with our parents when he had a late shift and I was still allowed to go. You said it lightly, jokingly, but I could feel that it was forced by the way it came out between your teeth.

"Cam brought me to the docks again," I to you, cheerfully, and watched your features flicker and rearrange themselves as your suspicions were confirmed. I had all the time in the world, it seemed – as long as it wasn't with you.

"That boy is full of surprises," your dad gave you a sidelong glance, arched one eyebrow in a way that was such a mirror image of you that I couldn't help but smile.

"I'm sure you could come with sometime," I didn't sound truthful even to myself, but I kicked you gently anyway and you kicked back.

Before, these dinners had been constructed entirely of arms crisscrossing with passed dishes, voices rising and falling over each other and laughter catching us all. It was still there, sometimes – just barely under the surface of the vacant conversations that lead nowhere and did nothing to drive us in any direction, much less forward. We could feel these stolen moments slipping away, and yet none of us seemed to know quite what to do to stop it. It was easier to stop planning than it was to make excuses for why we were all suddenly too busy every evening.

"And how is Cam doing these days?" your mom asked, and collectively the table became fascinated with their food.

"He's really good. Work has been settling down. He's around a lot more," I locked eyes with her, a challenge, and she only smiled.

"That's good. Maybe he can child-proof the house," she let one corner of her mouth twitch upward, and you choked on your burger and smothered the cough with your fist.

"Mom," you admonished, as your dad clapped one hand on your back.

"What?" she winked at me, as though I didn't know what

she was getting at, as if we weren't aware of the line we were toeing, "I just mean because Wren seems to be particularly accident prone these days."

This earned a relieved chuckle from the table, and none of them noticed that her gaze never faltered, that she kept her focus on me the entire time.

I see you, she said, without so much as a sound. I saw Penny's hand grip her shoulder briefly as she passed by on her way to the kitchen a few moments later, and something deep inside me curled up tighter.

In retrospect, this was an easy out, a *you can talk to us*, clearly a soft-edged confrontation. But in the moment, in the midst of my Cameron-induced haze, I saw it as anything but.

Because this was exactly what he had warned me about, on our way from the last dinner. Your mom didn't like him. Penny didn't like him. Our dads only tolerated him, and you seemed perpetually suspicious, perpetually on edge.

"They don't want you to be with me," he said bitterly, and when I reached out to touch his arm he hardly seemed to notice, "I can tell. They're going to try to get you to break it off."

"They wouldn't. They want me to be happy," I soothed, and he shot me a flicker of a somber smile, "and I'm happy with you."

"They won't tell you outright," he cautioned, "but you'll be able to tell, if you look for it. You can say 'I told you so' if I turn out to be wrong – but I know I'm not."

I don't have to explain to you how this works, right? Everyone else seems to have understood the entire time what was happening, though not how deep it went. Was I really so easily fooled, so easily swayed? I was so quick to turn on all of you – to let myself believe that he was the one being wronged from the start.

But no, I hadn't noticed, so I didn't say anything. Because it seemed, suddenly, that I had become an expert at not noticing what was so obvious to everyone else.

Doug and Penny were afraid, always afraid, to say anything that might cause them to lose me, though I have always done my best to make sure they know that they could never bring it upon themselves. I've failed them in more ways than that.

But your mom was never afraid. She didn't care if she ruffled feathers as long as we knew where she stood. She didn't care how mad she made me, as long as I knew, someday, where to find her. That's the kind of scrappy parenting your mom has always been so good at. She'll rile you up as much as possible, but she'll never make you feel unintelligent – just seen.

I was so angry at her, then. I get it now.

I'm sure you did all along,
Wren

54

The Great Love of My Life,

I sometimes get a little sad when I look at you; specifically on those bronze afternoons when we're done unwinding and have come completely undone.

We're loose-limbed and soft-breathed and I can see everything in you that makes so much sense to me. Because it's always been you, Sawyer, just like it's always been me, but that doesn't matter because it has never been us anyway. I look at you and there's a burning in my lungs and a clenching beneath my ribcage and I cannot comprehend the words I would need to explain it to you.

Maybe there are no words, because I truly and honestly believe that so many of the things that I feel are exclusive to me, no matter how well you may understand them for yourself.

Some part of me has always been convinced (so I can't even blame it fully on him – either 'him', any 'him') that nobody I know is ever completely honest with me. They know what I need to hear and so they say it – maybe it's not entirely dishonest, and maybe it's only ever with the best of intentions, but it is manipulative all the same, because the ending is for them to get what they want (even if what they want is for me to be happy). Is that seeing the worst in people? I don't think I've ever been broken enough to feel the way I do, and yet.

When your lips brush against my forehead and I lean into it like I want you to breathe me in – when the way we are makes people arch their eyebrows at me from afar. I feel like I need more but I don't *want* it. It doesn't make sense that I can't just choose, that we can't choose for ourselves how to feel and who to feel it for.

Anyone else (as if there has ever been, will ever be anyone I love quite like you who loves me quite like this) couldn't understand that I genuinely don't mean anything by it – I can't love you and you can't love me the right way and so instead we are something so much more genuine. You just love me and I just love you and sometimes when I look at you, I am reminded what it is to be heartsick and why it is they call it that.

I love you I love you,
Wren

55

Sawyer,

  I told you that he started the fire, but I never got a chance to explain how I knew.

  The morning had been years long; the three of us huddled together on the back bumper of the ambulance, the black smoke greying and eventually paling entirely as ashy sludge trickled down the yard and into the curb. The firemen said they were lucky – only the garage had sustained significant damage, and because of the breezeway between it and the house, none of their belongings inside would be lost to the smoke. I looked at the sagging paneling by the front door and the charred remains of Penny's lovingly-maintained flowerbeds, the way she sunk into Doug like she couldn't bear her own weight anymore, and I said *yeah, lucky.*

  It was ruled accidental, though nobody gave us a solid explanation for what the accident was.

  Your parents offered their spare room to mine until faulty wiring or any other possibly-recurring factors could be ruled out, and Cam made a face like the whole situation was just too much for him and insisted we go home so that I could rest off some of the stress. You locked eyes with me briefly from across the kinetic tangle that was our combined families, your brow furrowed just slightly, and then Cam looked up and you averted your gaze with practiced fluidity. I could feel your eyes on our backs as he steered me toward the car, hot and pointed as they combed my skin for any sign of retribution for my absence.

"Really unfortunate," Cam said, his fingers grazing my neck as he backed out of his parking spot, glancing at you over his shoulder, "but it could have been much worse. They're lucky."

I nodded mutely, still a little dazed and not yet having picked up on the shockwaves of energy coming off his skin.

"They said it could have been anything. A series of events. A coincidence."

"Yeah."

"Are you worried?"

I lifted my face slowly, turning toward him.

"About what?"

"That it could happen again," he said, after a brief pause during which he stared straight ahead and kept his jaw tight, "or just in general. It would make sense."

"They're safe," I pulled my legs up, wrapping my arms around them and resting my chin against my knees, "that's what matters."

He started to speak again, but seemed to think better of it, making a show of opening his mouth and closing it again. I knew he expected a reaction, but instead I pretended not to see, my eyes fixed on a chip in the corner of the windshield.

When we got back to the house, he waited for me to unfold myself and close the door behind me before resting his hand on the small of my back and guiding me toward the house. There was a feeling under my skin like I wasn't exactly part of my own body anymore, my bones murmuring in response to his proximity and my nerves beginning to hum at the arch of his neck.

"Why don't you go upstairs and get some rest," he emptied the contents of his pockets into the bowl on the end table, unfastened his watch and then lifted his hand slowly to brush my hair back from my face. When I didn't respond, he cupped my chin in his fingers and lifted until I raised my eyes to meet his.

"Okay," I said, obediently, because every second that I stood beside him made the hair on the back of my neck prickle and my muscles wind tighter, and because I suddenly felt the adrenaline that had been buzzing through my veins leave me in a flurry and replace itself with an exhaustion like nothing I'd ever felt before.

"I'll come check on you in a minute, alright?" he waited for me to nod unsteadily, "it could have been anything, sweetheart. That doesn't mean it's going to happen again. It could have been a kid playing around with fire and it got out of hand, it could have been someone dropping their cigar when it wasn't quite finished burning yet. Accidents happen, you know?"

"Yeah," I felt like I was sleepwalking, the ringing in my bones growing louder until it started to block out the sound of him talking, "I'm going to take a nap."

I pulled the blankets over me and up to my chin without even changing out of my jeans. Downstairs, Cam hummed to himself as he moved around in the kitchen, a cup clanking and the knob on the sink squeaking. The sound of my own heartbeat was deafening.

When he came upstairs to check on me, I forced my breathing to slow and let my eyes flicker under my lids, trying not to flinch when he smoothed the blanket and tucked the edges around me. He perched on the edge of the bed, his hand resting on my shoulder.

"It's a good thing you were here for them," he said softly, his voice gentle and even, "imagine if you hadn't come back and this had happened – it could have been so much worse."

I waited until I heard his footsteps trail back down the stairs before I opened my eyes again, my stomach churning.

His hands patting against his jeans and dropping his wallet into the silver dish with his keys. Cameron, who had never smoked a day in his life, removing an open package of cigarettes from his pocket, setting it upright with the same deliberation with which he did everything else, eyes meeting mine briefly but steadily.

Imagine if you hadn't come back. It could have been so much worse.

It could have been,
Wren

56

Sawyer,

About three weeks after I went to Ed, he showed up at the house.

I didn't answer the door, since I was sporting a fairly fresh black eye. And I didn't make it all the way down the stairs, either; I was on the third step from the top when they both looked up at me, mirror images of disgust and disdain, and I immediately tiptoed in reverse back out of sight.

Just around the corner, my back to the wall, I routed my possible ways out of the house. I could climb out onto the porch roof. Dangle from the bedroom window and hope I could land properly and limp off before they noticed. If they went into the kitchen, and I was quiet, I could have a chance to make it out the back door unseen.

I could already see it happening – Ed telling him about our discussion, standing guard on the front steps while Cam pounded his way up the stairs. I could practically feel the heat of his fury coming ahead of him.

Which is why what happened next surprised me so much.

"What the hell is the matter with you, huh? That's the first thing I see when I walk in the door?"

"We didn't plan on having company," Cam snapped back, but with much less bite than I usually received.

"Did you plan on her just never leaving the house again? Or

was that shiner an impulse decision?"

The ringing in my ears disappeared with a *whoosh*, a thick silence replacing it. Somewhere, I was aware of them arguing in low tones, still only a few feet from the front door, but the words evaded me. Surely he wasn't here to defend me? To try and hold his son accountable?

Why was I always caught off guard, always second-guessing? I like to think that I was a good judge of character at some point – I had you, after all – but at some point my radar had started spinning wildly and never stopped.

There was a muffled thud followed by a louder one, and I jolted forward, ducking around the doorway into the bathroom. My attempt to stay out of sight was pointless – neither of them would have noticed if I'd started doing cartwheels down the steps. Ed had shoved his son up against the wall, and it was clear by the fear and the color in Cam's face (so similar to my own) that the first sound I'd heard had been his fist connecting with face.

I closed the door with well-practiced silence, then turned and flushed the toilet, listening carefully as the tussle downstairs came to an immediate stop. As I splashed water on my face, the front door slammed, and a heavy quiet settled over the house. The only sound was that of his footsteps, slowly approaching.

He opened the door as I patted my skin dry, standing wordlessly before me, his eyes vacant. The blow had landed hard – there was a thin split along the sharp edge of his cheekbone. Mechanically, I opened the mirror and pulled out my usual supplies. He leaned one hip against the countertop, unfocused as I wiped the cut and applied the butterfly bandage with a skill he had allowed me to perfect.

He made eye contact with me as I finished, swiping the

wrappings into the trash.

"Thanks," he said, and I nodded once, averting my eyes, which only made him more insistent, "no, I mean it. Thank you."

There was something in his expression, something that I could almost interpret as genuine remorse. His gaze dropped from my eyes to the dark shadow beneath the left one, and the crease between his brows deepened.

"It's fine," I said automatically, almost defensively, "it doesn't hurt anymore."

We stood there in silence for another minute, and his thumb brushed so close that my eyelids fluttered.

"I'm sorry," he whispered, and something in me tilted just on the edge of breaking.

"It's okay," I lied. Did I know I was lying? Did I believe it? I don't know.

"Do you think," he paused, his fingers still tracing the planes of my face, "do you think – if it doesn't hurt too much – do you think you could cover it up?"

And I fell back into myself, sharp and all at once.

"Right now?"

"Yeah," his voice was still calm, but it grew immediately stronger, "I just... I can't look at it, you know? I look at it and it just makes me feel so guilty. I don't do this to you on purpose. Do you get that? I hate what you... I hate what happens when we fight. And it's so hard to move forward when it's staring me right in the face."

Silence. Silence. Silence. The next ten minutes, ten hours, ten days balancing on the next words out of my mouth. The crease of his frown. The continuous pulsing ache in the recesses of my brain.

"Yeah, of course," I said, my mouth twisting into some horrific flickering semblance of a smile, "I can cover it up."

He pressed a quick kiss to my forehead, rubbed my shoulder roughly as he slipped past me and slowed in the doorway. I waited, raising my eyes to meet his.

But he just smiled, eyes brighter than the last fifteen minutes should allow, and left me standing with my back to my reflection in the slanting light of the afternoon.

Your Friendly Neighborhood Makeup Artist,
Wren

57

Sawyer,

    I've been thinking about Luminol and how I imagine the inside of my car would light up like a city skyline.

    Of course, the seats are black, and I'm well versed in blood cleanup, but depending on how long that sort of thing works for, it might appear that I've died several times in that vehicle.

    The steering wheel, for sure, and the seatbelt as well. The pedals, headrest, handles. From split lips and bloodied noses and an unexpected shove that ricocheted my head off the passenger side window and reopened what was then a relatively fresh wound on my temple.

    Not to mention that I drove myself to you, all the times that weren't severe enough for the ER but were too severe to deal with on my own.

    Maybe I have died several times, because surely I am not the same person as I was before.

    It's not true that all of the cells in your body replace themselves after seven years. In seven years, there will still be parts of me that are the same as when he touched me last. All of the neurons in my cerebral cortex will be the same as when he locked me in the bathroom for two days, as when he kissed me, as when he lied.

    But they'll also be the same as when I saw the ocean for the first time, sharp and unending and bitter on my tongue, as the look on your face when I presented you with concert tickets to that indie band you briefly loved, as the night Doug and Penny sat down and presented me with adoption papers.

Maybe my skin is someone different every time I shower, or my lungs are new each time I stand alone in the sand and breathe in the endless salty expanse of the sea.

But if parts of me can die off and be replaced with someone new, then they can do it again and again and again until I'm something even better.

Love, Wren

58

The Great Love of My Life,

    I'm sure you've wondered periodically (if not continuously) throughout these letters what my actual reason is for writing them.

    After all, I am incredible at presents of all kinds, and they usually don't involve in-depth descriptions of me being beaten or my exact thought process when you and I fought.

    This isn't just the story you asked for, Sawyer, and it isn't just me showing you the world through my eyes.

    This is a timeline. It's all the holes in the proof that you've seen.

    Six weeks ago, in March, when you and your dad went on a trip to North Carolina to check out new lifts for the garage, something changed.

    He's getting worse, Sawyer. You might need this.

    I don't know how he found out about the IUD, but he did. Maybe he guessed and the look on my face was what confirmed it for him. Regardless, I had made a decision about my body without consulting him (ignoring, of course, that the IUD was a direct response to him making decisions about my body without consulting *me*).

    There was the usual one-sided argument, me getting cornered, the first blows falling. But this was different. This was so much worse than ever before. He didn't stop when he'd gone too far, or when he'd worked it out of his system. He *didn't stop.*

The entire day is foggy to me now, which is probably as a result of blacking out multiple times and never getting the necessary medical treatment, but I remember waking up alone in the kitchen, surrounded by what seemed like an impossible amount of my own blood.

I don't know what he did to me, because every inch of my body hurt and every inch of me seemed to *be* hurt.

He left. Packed a bag and vanished without a trace.

After over five years and covering for him every time he'd wronged me, he thought he'd gone too far, and he bailed.

Of course, I didn't know that yet. I just assumed he'd gotten tired of me and gone to bed.

I thought I was going to die. I didn't know how I hadn't already. I was so pathetic, Sawyer, that I dragged myself only a few feet away and let myself fall back asleep without even trying to call for help, or to figure out where all of the blood was coming from.

When I woke up again, it was dusk, the room filled with hazy orange light and arrant dust particles. I peeled myself off the floor (literally – I was adhered to it), my bones shifting and crackling with each inch of movement.

I called out for him, but my voice got caught behind my teeth and I tilted forward, vomiting across the already stained wood laminate flooring.

I don't know how long I waited for him to come back, or how long it took me to get all the way from the kitchen to the bathroom down the steps, but I do know that by the time I had the sun had long since disappeared beneath the horizon and the house was still deathly quiet except for the strangled noises I was making in my attempts to get from point A to point B.

I slept again on the bathroom floor, and by some miracle (or lack thereof) I woke up once more with moonlight painting blue stripes across my skin. Again, blood had pooled beneath me, but this puddle was significantly smaller and of less concern to me than the black spots in my vision. I tugged myself free of my clothes and somehow managed to get myself over the lip of the bath and get the water running, where it swirled dark and unforgiving down the drain. I lay there, motionless, until the water ran cold, and then for awhile after, when I found the strength to push the tab and cut off the flow.

I couldn't even get a towel until the water still clinging to my skin had chilled me enough to numb some of the pain, and even then it was a slow and unsteady trip from the tub to the cupboard. With the blood gone, I could see the expanse of bruises spread across my body, but the pulsing in my head made it clear even the extensive damage before me was nothing compared to my face. I could already taste the blood running from my forehead down my nose and catching on my lips.

It was when the sun started rising on me, still wrapped in a towel in the fetal position on the bathroom floor, that I realized he was gone.

I considered calling you, but I couldn't remember where I'd put my phone and I didn't have the energy to go looking. I could hardly even make it back up the stairs, where the sight in the kitchen brought me back to my knees and finally all the way to the ground, sitting against the wall and trying not to cry because the salt stung my face.

He was usually careful about keeping the damage hidden.

I slept again at the foot of the stairs, and then once more at the top after pulling myself up them deemed me unfit to go any further. When I got to the bedroom, I noticed his dresser drawers hanging open, his side table emptied. Shivering, my hair still damp and most of my skin left uncovered by the towel, I sat down in front of the full-length mirror on the closet door and tried to survey the damage.

A few of my teeth felt loose in my mouth (he's since had them replaced). My nose, already compromised from the first break last June, was crooked again (he's since had it rebroken and reset), my eyes rimmed by dark shadows that were only accented by the blood running from the swollen gash crossing my temple and arching over my forehead (you saw this one, after guessing that bangs weren't just because I thought a new hairstyle would be fun). My lip was split and swollen, and two handprints circled my neck, thumbs dark in the hollow of my throat.

Two broken ribs, which healed on their own. A fractured collar bone, which, thanks to neglect, also did (but it aches from time to time). Bruising and swelling distorted the shape and color of my limbs, my bones seeming to jut purple from my skin. Thin red lines made random patterns over my hips and thighs. I traced them and saw a flickering memory (nightmare?) of him kneeling over me, tears in his eyes, hissing angry promises. The whites of my eyes were streaked with crimson, and a smattering of maroon freckles dusted my cheeks.

I see my reflection in my nightmares still.

I slept, restless and yet too exhausted to move, and lost track of time. Over the course of the next 24 hours, I got dressed, and got to my feet, and bandaged what I could. Somehow, I made my way back to the kitchen.

Some deep, mechanical part of my brain started going through the motions. Towels. Bleach. Sitting half on my knees, one hand clutched to my side, the other working rhythmically at the dark stain on the floor, coming up with excuses. I spent hours there, stopping only to rest my head against the cool metal of the refrigerator door, arms curled around myself. I scrubbed until the pool had faded into a faintly rust-colored shadow, and my fingers were cracked and burning from the bleach.

He'd be angry, when he came back. He'd be furious to see the mess I'd made, and how impossible it would be to clean up.

I realized there was no disappearing this, and it occurred to me suddenly that it could be weeks before anybody even realized anything was wrong. I had alienated you; I'd made you grow accustomed to long periods without sight nor sound of me, and you knew better than to come looking.

He'd trained me well, Sawyer, and in turn, without thinking, without realizing, I had done the same to you.

I cleaned, and I bandaged, and I rested, lying still and cold as a corpse on my side of the bed, arms at my sides, waking abruptly every time I moved so much as an inch. Days passed. The pain dulled to a constant ache that throbbed with every breath.

Still it evades me how I woke up every time. How I woke up at all. How the fragments that I'm made up of didn't fall apart completely and take me with them.

I don't know why I didn't try to call you. I don't know why I didn't call anyone. I didn't even look for my phone; instead I wandered the house, battered and hollow, until my hobble turned into a limp which turned into a shuffle, until changing the dressings on my wounds each day stopped turning up so much fresh blood and a whole colorful array of stains.

He must have been watching the news, wherever he was. Watching and waiting, biding his time, wondering how long it would be before someone found me, how long before they connected it to him.

Panicking, because it would be impossible for them not to.

His curiosity must have caught up to him, because he came back. I was sitting on the floor at the end of the kitchen table, having pulled up all of the ruined segments of faux-wood paneling and piled them next the trash, a stained, gaping hole left in the center of the kitchen floor. I heard his key in the lock, hesitant, cautious, and my blood ran cold.

He entered hastily, guiltily, keeping his back to the room and his eyes on the yard, bolting the door and giving the already-closed curtains a reassuring tug. And then he turned around to face the ghost standing before him.

I had been numb, Sawyer, in his absence. I hadn't cried – not really, not if you didn't count the few tears that leaked out as I sucked air through my teeth and poured rubbing alcohol into my open skin. But when I saw him, the color gone from his face, his eyes wide and his mouth agape, I dissolved.

There was no coming back from this one, but we didn't seem to realize it yet. He crossed the distance between us quickly, dropping his bag and his keys, but stopped abruptly a few inches away. My breath was uneven, a sob caught in the back of my throat, and when he reached out, his hand feather-light on my bruised cheek, I unraveled into his arms like he'd taught me to.

"It's okay, it's okay," he whispered into my hair as I wept, lowering both of us to the ground and pulling me onto his lap. I sobbed into his chest and he rocked me, swaying, murmuring into my hair, "I'm here, sweetheart, everything's going to be alright."

Even knowing what he had done, even fearing him with every fiber of my being, I still eased into him, craving the contact, needing the gentleness and the coolness of his fingers on my skin.

I cried, and he held me while I came undone.

"It's okay, Wren," he soothed, his hand cradling the nape of my neck, the other brushing my hair back from my damp skin, "I'm not mad about the mess."

I know,
Wren

59

Sawyer,

I'm sorry.

If you couldn't read it, if you can't, if you want to burn it and hope that it also burns it out of the inside of your eyelids, I understand. I wish I could unfeel it. I wish I could explain to everyone how I feel and how it's been to feel this way for so long without them ever having to really understand it.

Do you understand now, why I can't just leave? Why it's not safe for you, not safe for Doug and Penny, not safe for your parents or for CJ or for anyone in the shop? Where is he going to direct the unbridled rage he would usually reserve for me if I am both the cause and unable to receive it? You still have dinner with your parents once a week at least, Sawyer. That's not a flaw, but it's an arrow pointing straight to your Achilles heel.

I can disconnect. I've done it before. I can tell myself, and mostly believe it, that my parents and yours and you would all be fine and better off without me. That you've been okay before and you'll be okay again. But Sawyer, I am not so sure that they would be without you.

Once, I would have had no doubt about it. But I have found a home here – within all of you – in a way that I never would have believed possible. And so maybe it's my weakness, too. It wouldn't be a bad one to have.

But I need someone to understand. I need someone to see

why I have stayed all this time, why I've done next to nothing and let myself fall deeper and deeper. I no longer trust my own judgement, Sawyer, but I have trusted yours since the moment that scrap of paper landed on my desk and we made eye contact for the first time.

I know it's not fair to ask that of you. And that's why I'm putting it here – where I can feel I've shown you the best I can, and I can make my own assumptions from there. You don't have to say a word. Knowing that you know as much as I do and can still love me is enough.

Love, Wren

60

Sawyer,

There were always things I didn't tell you because I couldn't stand the look in your eyes.

It's all coming out now, isn't it? So I might as well.

He likes my hair darker. We have a schedule to keep ourselves maintained to his standards. To make ourselves so pretty that nobody will ever question our behavior.

I have appointments with hair stylists and face specialists and groomers and the gym. To keep me small but not strong. To keep me busy.

He does what he can to airbrush real life.

But these are things I didn't tell you, because it took longer for anyone to realize that I was getting worse while looking better.

Because even when it was for all the wrong reasons, only physical, only external, I still basked in your compliments, in your elbow tickling my ribcage and your temple nearly grazing mine as you whispered, "looking good, Chickadee." I still stood a little taller, found myself smiling a little brighter, when I entered a room to a course of parental, 'look at you's.

You only ever wanted me to be happy. To be safe. To be healthy. And I was, when I was with you. He made me up to conceal the poison he was pumping through my veins, when I could have made it there on my own if he'd just let me.

Well, maybe not all the way there. Apparently being

effortlessly pretty is fairly expensive.

And I still told you more than I told anyone else. The last time we ever had dinner with Doug and Penny, she caught me at the door when Cam was already halfway across the lawn. I faltered, watching how his shoulders tensed, his gaze zeroing in on where her hand rested on my arm.

"Are you happy?" she asked, and I could see in her eyes how desperately she wanted to never have the question in her mind in the first place.

I could have told her. I opened my mouth to do it, knowing full well that she'd have me inside with the door shut between us in an instant if I did.

But people change when they know things like this. If I told them – if I told your parents, if I told anyone else – then it became their pain, too. I couldn't let them carry it, but more exhaustingly, more thoroughly, I couldn't bear the weight of their own grief on top of my own. And so I said nothing at all.

I smiled, weakly and with a little head tilt to imply that I hadn't quite heard the question, and then I leaned in for one more quick hug and nearly sprinted across the grass to where he was waiting.

No part of me even entertained the idea that asking for help would save me. My mind was always ten steps ahead of each decision I made, but still somehow ten steps behind his.

Because she could close the door, she could call for help, and at the end of the day I knew that it wouldn't make a difference. Every path, no matter how tangled or twisted, lead back to him. And every path that involved asking for help meant living with the knowledge that I was consciously hurting them, too.

Believe me, I know now how deeply flawed my reasoning

was. It still is, sometimes. But it all felt so real, Sawyer. When someone has woven themselves into the very fabric of your life, it's easy for them to pull a few strings.

Conversations he swore never happened until I felt them blurring in my memory. Bruises he seemed not to recall until I explained them away to myself. Smaller things, like kitchen appliances moving in the cupboards from day to day, articles of clothing going missing, jewelry disappearing and then showing up again overnight. It was like looking in a mirror and noticing that your features were all changing on their own, until you weren't quite sure what your face actually looked like.

I don't like my reflection, Sawyer. She is beautiful, and unrecognizable, and I hate her guts.

Thank you for loving even the ugly insides of me.

-*Wren*

61

Sawyer, Sawyer, Sawyer,

Something about being sixteen and wild and tumultuous feels nostalgic, even though you couldn't pay me enough to go back to then.

Because even though things have clearly grown wildly beyond my control, being a teenager is only so great in retrospect.

The nights we spent down by the water, our classmates howling and cannonballing and making mistakes at lightning speed just out of our line of sight, we felt so much older and wiser than we really were. Maybe it was just in comparison to the riffraff we were surrounded by, but I'm sure it also had a lot to do with our continuously inflating egos.

People got into messes, and our proximity to each other made everything everyone's business. Somehow, the people next to you knew every mistake you'd ever made, and you knew all of theirs, but nobody ever seemed to talk about it. Parents brushed DUIs and possession charges under the rug. The cops flashed their lights and chirped their sirens at the suspicion of underaged drinking instead of attempting to put a stop to it.

"I only quit smoking because it got too expensive," I told you, and, bless your heart, you only looked startled for a second, "that and I left that home. It kept them away from me when I smelled like an ashtray."

I prefer not to know things, because then I don't have to be disappointed. It's a near-constant state of being for me: continuous disappointment at the state of the world despite being shown again and again that it is exactly as ruthless as it has proven itself to be. Some part of me still wants to believe that the people around me can do no wrong – that the people I choose to surround myself with are just as perfect as I see them.

You're just the opposite. You want to know all the gritty dirty raw stuff, so that there are no surprises. That's probably for the best – ignorance has never really brought me bliss.

We are both very skilled at hiding our thoughts. At first, I would blurt out things like my abandoned chain-smoking endeavor or my habit of pushing back the cuticle on my thumb until it bled, waiting to see your eyes flicker or your shoulders shift. When my abrasive truths were met only with acceptance, they started rolling out smoother, quieter, more earnestly. I had learned to smother my emotions because they showed weak spots, and that made me easy to manipulate. You kept yours level because that was how you made sure nobody ever felt small under your gaze.

And so being sixteen with you was the best being sixteen could have been. I look back on it and remember it like the upbeat movie montage it so clearly wasn't, but you're in every scene. You look at me, and your voice dips lower, your eyes get softer around the edges. I loved being sixteen with you because it was the first time I ever felt like I was home.

Sixteen was the first time that things had real consequence, real weight. Everything bad was still the worst thing that had ever happened to us – not because of raging emotions and dramatics but just because we had yet to experience anything else.

But everything good was also still the best. I snuck out of my room in the night and soared across the yard like a dart, meeting our friends (and, of course, you) in the shadows for no other reason than to wander the streets aimlessly until the sky started turning navy or a deputy drove by too slowly too many times. I'd slip back into bed just in time for Penny to shuffle out of their room, my heart pounding in the space between my eyes and my nerves zinging. Everything was so much more alive inside of me.

When I think of sixteen, I think of laughing so hard my ribs ache, of falling asleep in the passenger seat of your car, of everything being sharp-edged and technicolor.

It really wasn't so great; I remember that in the next moment.

Doug and Penny have no idea how much of my relationship with them hinged on you. They adored you from day one – even when they didn't have me, and therefore had no reason to love you; they loved you in advance, because you were there, and you were you and maybe they just knew. I never had that. Until them, until you, until your parents, I'd never had love, period, much less love that wasn't conditional. But affection was habitual to you, to your parents, and to mine even before they knew me. Imagine that. Habitual love.

That's not to say you're perfect – get that out of your smug little head right this instant. You're not nearly as far from it as I am, but I'm only obligated to give you so much praise a day, and my love isn't as instinctive as yours.

But you were raised in a house that said "I love you" like it wasn't even a thought; you loved them, and they loved you and that was just the way it was. I think knowing me has helped you realize what a truly amazing thing that is – to have people that you love so casually that you don't even need to think about it. But, likewise, knowing you has taught me that saying it doesn't wear it out. I can love people just as much as they love me, and I'm not going to use it

up. There isn't a finite amount of love in the world.
If there was, we'd really be burning through it.

I love you indefinitely,
Wren

After

62

TO: dawnmoore@mooreauto.com ; terrymoore@mooreauto.com
FROM: sawyermoore@mooreblogs.com
SUBJECT: Passive Aggressive

  Since I promised I'd write at least twice a week, even though you can read nearly everything I'm doing on the blog and I'm an adult so you can't make me promise anything anymore, here's my update:

  I finally left Salt Lake City this morning, headed back toward home in a zigzag so that I can catch all of the obscure tourist attractions you never wanted to stop at when we made these trips in my youth. Don't worry – I'm only a little bitter.

  Once I get home I'm going to have to make more wrens; I've been leaving them everywhere she wanted to visit, and with all the owners of the tiny houses I've stopped to see. A lot of them haven't even heard of her. It's getting a little easier to talk about. But I've only got a few left. To be completely honest, that's part of the reason I'm stopping home again. I've still got the entire northeast to explore, but I'll probably wait until summer to head up that way because one midwestern winter was more than enough for me.

  I've been updating my blog every week (also just like I told you I was going to!!!! Incredible!) and believe it or not, I *am* still getting a decent amount of traffic. And hardly anyone comments calling me a cold-blooded murderer anymore, so that's refreshing (that was a joke, mom. They usually just call me a regular murderer).

I guess you were both right that it was mostly just gawkers, because hits have dropped significantly since they stopped airing that ridiculous "documentary" every five seconds. There's a new surge of traffic every time any of us are mentioned on TV, but they seem to lose interest pretty quickly once they realize there's no news for them here. I think I make them sad. That's okay; they make me sad, too.

Tonight I'm staying in a motel awhile outside of Denver, and I'll probably be on the road again before eight. There's so much to see, and so few people to see it with! I'm making lots of friends – everyone traveling out here is more than happy to share their days with a stranger. Don't worry, I'm being smart and I'm scarier than all of them, anyway.

I'll be home within the month. I'll write again on Friday.

All the love in the world,
Sawyer

TO: sawyermoore@mooreblogs.com
FROM: cjturner@anymail.com
SUBJECT: Re: Playing Telephone

Hey again,

Missed your call, and when I tried to call you back it went straight to voicemail. Service is spotty in the middle of nowhere, I suppose.

When will you be home next? I'm still living large in NJ at the moment (rent's cheaper than it is across the bridge), but I'll be back in town around the holidays. It'd be good to see you for once.

(Yes, your mom emailed me – but I'd have liked to see you regardless.)

Take care of yourself, bud. By all means, do what you gotta do – but at the end of the day I'll still expect to see you in Clearwell come Christmas.

Your turn to call,

CJ

TO: cjturner@anymail.com
FROM: sawyermoore@mooreblogs.com
SUBJECT: Re: Playing Telephone

Bro,

How can it be my turn to call again? Is it really anybody's turn if nobody ever answers the phone?

I found a note taped to the underside of my passenger seat yesterday. Stuff from her just keeps turning up and part of me is afraid every time that it's going to be the last. Because eventually it has to be the last, right?

I'm taking care of myself. A vegetable a day and all that. See you at Christmas.

When do you get off work anyway?

Sawyer

63 - Sawyer

According to several witnesses, I'd been the last one to see her alive. There were no records indicating any sort of domestic abuse, but there were records that, once upon a time, I'd shown up at their house snarling and swinging and shouting loud enough for the whole neighborhood to hear.

Where I was angry, Cameron was calm. Where I was pacing and calling every official I could, he was bowing his head for the cameras and asking that his fiancé be brought back home.

Sheriff Stone may have handed off the investigation to the state police immediately, but he never once took himself out of the equation.

Almost immediately after the police arrived at my door for the first time, we started hearing murmurings of search warrants. Stone, likely under the guidance of his son, slipped hints that sent the prosecution sniffing my way.

I would have been an easy win for them; I was jealous, sly, seemingly aimless in contrast to Cam's apparent earnestness and determination. Her belongings, left scattered amongst mine, proclaimed infidelity to anyone who didn't know us. Her blood was in my car, my apartment, the garage.

But I was also cooperative. I went willingly to the station, sat hunched in stiff-backed chairs at tables that froze confessions out of even the innocent. I helped them write out timelines, filled in gaps and falterings in Cam's stories with the truth.

At first, they were only concerned with her whereabouts. Was she safe? Was she hurt? Was she gone of her own accord, or had she been snatched away like so many wide-eyed young women before her, destined to be remembered only by the same handful of carefully-selected photos that would slowly flicker out of news programs as the months progressed? Cam and his father both insisted on my involvement, pushing the edges of the truth until it began to blur into something else entirely.

So I told them what I knew. That she had been scared, terrified, desperate, even angry, yes. But that she had no concrete plans, no escape route.

"She went to the cops on more than one occasion," I told them, and interrupted before they could say what I knew was on the tips of their tongues, "but no, there won't be any reports."

Their interest in me faded almost instantaneously when they gained access to his house and, by some miraculous chain of circumstances, pulled up the floorboards in the kitchen.

But away with their interest in me went anyone's hopes of finding her alive.

They looked for a murder weapon, but I knew they were both at the ends of his wrists.

Most of the evidence had been scrubbed away by the time they combed his house. They argued that much of what they did find was easily dismissed – blood found in the trim beneath the shower could have been a shaving accident, the fist-sized bruises fading quickly from Cameron's chest could have been from anything with how much time had passed.

In all the time I knew him, I'd never seen him squirm until the jury started to falter.

When they read off their verdict, none of them looking

Cameron in the eye or even in the face, there were no shouts of disbelief from the crowd. Nobody cried out, nobody gasped in shock. His father stood and left the room, looking more disgusted than horrified and letting the door slam shut behind him. Her parents kept their chins raised and jaws set despite the tears streaming openly down their cheeks. There was no satisfaction in the eyes of those who had come to see him locked away.

But here's the thing: I'm guilty, too.

All throughout the investigation, all throughout the trial, I knew about the car. I knew about the lockbox under the seat. I knew that not only did she have a plan, I had provided her with an escape route.

I also knew that mentioning it would create a tsunami of reasonable doubt, and I'd be damned if I was going to be the reason he didn't spend the rest of his life behind bars.

So I lied on the stand. I stared my family and hers in the eyes and I told them I didn't know anything, so that they wouldn't have to do the same.

And in the end, it didn't help anyone, because she was still dead, and no amount of lying could bring her back.

64 - Sawyer

We looked for a body, at first.

I was allowed to join the search – over a hundred of us gathered in lines with fingertips nearly touching, ducking under Spanish moss and sidestepping dense foliage as we swept from the location of the car all the way back to the bay. Someone found her phone, half-buried in the packed sand and shattered into something nearly unrecognizable. Someone else shouted from upriver, and I found myself breaking ranks and shoving my way through anyone else who did, my heart clamoring up into the roof of my mouth.

Across the slow-moving water, a whole congregation of gators sunned themselves – more than I'd ever seen at once, much less so close to where we'd spent our teenage summers. As more of the search party arrived, the animals twitched and growled from deep in their throats.

"Sawyer," a woman nearby grabbed my elbow, and I swallowed heavily, clenching my teeth to steady my trembling jaw.

"How do we check?" I asked, loudly, and a few heads turned, "how do we check them?"

"No way in hell," a murmur made its way through the growing crowd, "there's no way."

"Why are they here, then?" my voice broke, and a few of the officers who'd joined us glanced at each other, "have any of you ever seen them so close to here? Some of us are here every week. Have you ever seen them so close?"

There was another shout, this time from the direction we'd come from, and when my head whipped around sharply, one of the officers reached out to me.

"Son, I think it's best you head on home."

"She's my best friend," I whispered, and I hated myself for being so weak almost as much as I hated him, "I can't just do nothing."

"Maybe she turns up," he patted my shoulder, averting his eyes as though the red rims of mine burned him, "maybe she'll come to you first, yeah? Home might be the best place for you to be right now."

He was lying through his teeth, and we both knew it. We both glanced at the gators, the crowd mumbling and whispering amongst themselves as the beasts hissed.

"She was wearing a grey t-shirt and jeans," I told him, unable to take my eyes off the water as though blinking would allow crucial evidence to slip past us, "when she came to see me that night, remember, that's what she was wearing. But if she came out later, if he brought her out here, she would have had a sweatshirt on. Probably black, maybe blue. Zippered. Lightweight."

The words that came out of his mouth were, "okay, son," but his eyes were only the first in a long line of faces that said "I'm so sorry for your loss".

65 - Sawyer

We'd been down to the bay a solid two-dozen times before she confessed that she'd never actually seen the ocean.

"I mean, the Gulf, obviously. So, I have. But only from the car, and only the once. And the Bay, but – "

The next morning we were loading up the back of my truck with beach towels and snacks and a monstrosity of an umbrella, while Penny watched from the front porch with a cup of coffee and paperback in hand.

It was a three-and-a-half-hour drive from her house to the sea. She started with her feet curled beneath her, feeding me chips and staring at me giddily until I'd turn my head just enough to lock eyes and earn a heartbreaking grin. The closer we got to our destination, the closer to the windshield she got, until her butt was barely even perched on the edge of the seat and her fingers were splayed out on the dashboard.

I loaded up my arms as she leapt from the cab, throwing the bag of towels over her shoulder and sprinting ahead of me up the wooden pathway, ponytail swinging, legs pumping.

"Wait up," I called, because I didn't make the trip not to see this, though the journey itself was part of the fun.

She spun to face me, grabbing my wrist and tugging me forward as she backed toward the sound of crashing water.

And then there it was: vast and loud and yet somehow muted, her eyes widening and her hand falling from mine and the wind whipping her hair around her temples.

"Here's good," I said, my words sucked out of my mouth with the breeze, because she was already dropping her bag and kicking off her shoes and her eyes were fixated on the horizon, lips parted, chin raised.

Then she was off, the sand parting under her feet as she shimmied her shorts down her legs and flung her t-shirt out behind her, leaving a trail of fiery excitement in her wake. I watched as she came to a standstill right at the water's edge, as it rose up to meet her and then to pass her, swirling past the backs of her knees and licking at her fingertips. When she turned to face me, she kept her arms folded across her stomach, and I could tell her toes were curling despite not seeing them.

"Coming?" she called, squinting into the sun and squealing as I ran toward her, pulling her with me further in. We went down together in a tangle of limbs and salt and sharp inhales as we broke through the surface, water fluttering on her lashes as she blinked.

"Well?" I asked, as she steadied her feet and smoothed her hair back from her face with one hand.

"Everyone on Earth lives on an island."

After a brief pause, she turned to look up at me, her fingers still curled around the crook of my elbow.

"Thanks for driving me all the way to the ocean."

"Thanks for giving me a reason to drive all the way to the ocean."

What I meant was *thanks for being my reason*, but while we had already decided on what we were to each other, she seemed much more comfortable with the intense stuff than I was just yet.

Later, when we'd swum ourselves lazy and settled into the lukewarm sand, she still watched the ocean and I still watched her.

She laid on her stomach with her elbows propping her up, ankles crossed and wrists folded under her chin; the sky changed colors like the slowest kaleidoscope, and her eyes followed every second of it.

She fell asleep on the drive home, which I knew she would even though she promised she wouldn't. Her head lolled against the glass, eyelashes dark against her cheeks, neon lights illuminating her skin and the ringlets salted into her hair.

We still had so much to say and so much to learn back then, before everything started unraveling. Her sandy toes curled into my knee as she tucked her legs up on the bench seat. I kept the music low.

"How was the ocean?" Doug asked as we made our way through the front door, her thumb hooked through my belt loop and her arm snaked around my waist as she leaned into me for support.

"Endless," she proclaimed sleepily, throwing one arm out for emphasis, shimmying her hip against mine, and he winked at me as she stood on tiptoes to press her bitter lips to my cheek, to whisper in my ear.

He turned out the lights behind her as she stumbled up the stairs, her fingers trailing along the banister and her eyes only half-open.

"Thank you," he told me, and almost said more, but instead just smiled and drifted into the dimly-lit kitchen, letting me see myself out.

The short drive home was silent and empty, and I stood under the spray of the shower until the water faded from scalding to frigid, my bones heavy and my muscles still warm.

I plugged my phone in as I climbed into bed, and paused when I saw her name on the screen.

Thank you. Every day.

I paused for a moment before responding, the glow of the screen blinding in the darkness, the words rearranging themselves in my bleary vision.

Love you too, Sparrow.

66 – Sawyer

I desperately want to want to be alone.

It seemed easier, at first, to steer clear of our parents and the weight with which their eyes fell on me. I had fallen far from the pedestal Wren had placed me on. I was tarnished.

Penny was all rage and fists and fire, descending upon me with the unrestrained hatred that she couldn't unleash on Cam. My mom was mostly silent, her jaw trembling at the sight of me and her head shaking almost involuntarily – as if even her subconscious was disappointed that I was her son.

Because none of it made sense anymore. How do you explain to the grieving parents that you thought you had it under control when you never really did? How do you tell them that you loved her too much to save her?

How do you justify to them what you can't even justify to yourself?

"I don't understand, Sawyer," they all kept saying – accusatory or confused or angry, "I don't understand why you didn't just come to us:"

Because of the fire. Because of the fear. Because she begged me not too, and, at some point, we had gone too far to come clean.

My dad didn't speak to me for two weeks after he found out.

"If she's dead, you helped dig her grave," Doug told me, solemnly, as he guided Penny away, "boy, you better hope she comes home."

It was different, after the trial. At the end of my first day on the stand, Penny let me fall into her arms as though I was the one who had been broken beyond repair.

'I know, sweetheart. I know now."

But you can't un-say things that come out in the heat of the moment. Their forgiveness didn't make me any less guilty, didn't shine me up again so I was worthy of it. There was always going to be a part of me that they blamed for their sun going out, even if they would never again admit it. And I don't apologize anymore, because it does more harm than good.

There's a picture in my dad's office of the two of them together at the Grand Canyon. Her arms are outstretched, one hand gripping his elbow in mock-fear while he holds her by the belt loop, both of them leaning precariously close to the edge. He keeps it on his desk with a birthday card she wrote for him, still tucked inside the envelope because it's his and his alone.

"You're still my son, Sawyer," he said as I packed up my car, "but she was my kid, too."

She was the only person that I wanted to talk to about the fact that she was gone, because she was the only person who could possibly have understood how I was feeling. We wouldn't even have had to speak. I talk to her alone in my car, mostly in my head but often out loud, and the silence rings in my ears just loud enough to pretend it's drowning out her responses and that's why I can't hear them. Sometimes it's companionable, other times I'm angry and so she is by extension. I reprimand myself for thinking that I loved her too much to help her when in reality I didn't love her enough to risk losing her – and so I did anyway, as anyone could have seen coming, as we should have seen coming. We were both childish and irresponsible and yet no matter how furious I am I can't bring myself to focus it in her direction. She has been punished enough. I never will be.

And so it's best to be alone, because nobody can grieve properly when the source of their misery is still kicking around miserably himself.

And it's best to be alone, because there is no more comfort that anyone can give me that can justify what we did, or didn't do, or fix what happened as a result.

67 - Sawyer

Six miles out of Hutchinson when the grinding grows too loud to ignore, I drop my car off and make my way across the street to a coffee shop. Ordering purely to use their Wi-Fi, I choose the furthest corner and shove both earbuds in, keeping my volume low and my shoulders hunched.

It doesn't really get any easier.

Even after six years, even after starting the adventure we were supposed to go on together, even driving through cities in Kansas with names like Hope and Paradise and Kismet and Home, there is a constant and undeniable absence that I carry with me everywhere I go.

This was her trip. She planned it, with neat little notes printed and passed to me in class, and texts sent in the middle of the night, and tucked into my back pocket when she'd leave again for undetermined amounts of time.

I expected catharsis at the very least. And I do feel it, sometimes, when I'm standing on the edge of the Grand Canyon or roaming the aisles at Powell's Books in Oregon or exceeding 120 on straight stretches through Montana where you can see everything in your path for miles. But catharsis is nothing compared to looking at the face of someone you love sitting next to you and knowing that they are experiencing the moment with as much intensity and weightlessness as you. It's nothing at all when it could be her, caught in the breeze, sunlight on her face and a smile on her lips, her eyes softening when they meet mine and I know she feels it, too.

The time before was harder than the trial itself; the not knowing and then the continuous onslaught of information that you could spend your entire life wishing to forget. Being a witness in a trial for the murder of someone who you'd seen sixteen and sprinting barefoot across the hot sand and into the sea, eighteen and finding you in the crowd to show you her diploma with such fierce joy in her eyes that it nearly brought tears to yours, twenty-one and sleeping on your couch through the best part because she insisted on watching a movie she had already seen three times – it drains the will out of you.

It's exhausting, waking up every day and answering endless questions about things you'd rather erase, knowing all the while that there are still people who will never believe your innocence.

All of this comes to a head when the judge asks you why she didn't just go to the police that night, and you answer, in front of your parents and her killer and a camera that will record you and replay you back to the world, "probably, your honor, with all due respect, because they'd done a really shitty job all the other times."

And then the trial was over and he was gone and there were no more distractions from her absence. It had been easier, with everything going on, to pretend that once it was over things would go back to normal and she'd still be around, kicking me under the table and playing cards in the shop with us on our breaks. I caved under the pressure of my parents and started seeing a therapist as soon as a verdict was reached, and it was her suggestion to donate Wren's funds we'd been stashing away to a program like Alexandra House. And maybe that would have been my catharsis, had I not found her drawer wiped clean except for the coffee can, which had also been emptied before it was placed back inside.

I still feel guilty for the way I turned on them, every last one of the guys I had worked with for years, who'd bonded with her just as quickly as they had with me, who'd contributed, who'd cared about her. I sent the can flying, careening off the hood of a car and rolling across the floor, the lid still in my hand, seething.

"Who the hell was in here? Did one of you take this? Which one of you took this?"

And the bitter sorrow in Shawn's voice when he spoke up first, "nah, man. We loved her, too."

It took me awhile to believe them, since they were the only ones who had known about it; and when I finally did it was only because I couldn't live with the idea that they would have done something like that after everything that had happened. I woke up with a jolt in the middle of the night and found myself digging through her favorite hiding places like I was losing my mind; when I came up with handfuls of notes she'd written and gifts I'd given her that she'd stashed away in my house for safekeeping, I started to think I was.

How can we stop looking? How can we be sure we can make this stick? How can we prosecute without a body?

Because nobody could have realistically lost that much blood and fought back, much less swim away. Because we found her engagement ring with his fingerprints on it hidden in the drawer in the kitchen. Because there was new vinyl flooring with blood and bleach underneath it and a call from her asking to come pick her car up – except when the company arrived there was no her or her car. Because when they found it, three days later, having been towed from a no-parking zone two miles outside Ochlockonee, it was wiped very nearly clean but not quite clean enough.

Because you knew he'd done it before and he'd gone too far. Because there's no other way it could have gone. Because she's just dead, Sawyer, we're so sorry.

It's really hard to keep friends when you're angry and bitter and never want to hang out. It's even harder when you're obsessed with closure that everyone's told you you're never going to get – even if you killed and gutted every alligator from Ochlockonee to the gulf you'd never find her body.

But he stood up and pointed and screamed in court that I was a liar, that I'd been jealous, that it was me. They'd already ruled me out and yet there he was, spit flying and face red and fists slamming against the table before him, sending papers flying and bailiffs lunging, "she was hardly even breathing when I left her, so where'd she go, Sawyer?"

Hammering the final nail into his coffin, leaving me shell-shocked and wide-eyed on film that was trimmed and zoomed in on and replayed on YouTube with hundreds of thousands of hits while the case grew larger.

Once I stopped being trailed every time I left the house by reporters or cops or random citizens, I drove north until I came to the garage, which looked exactly as we'd left it from the outside except for the vines starting to overtake the frame.

I pried a few tendrils off of the knob as I turned the key, holding my breath involuntarily and closing my eyes as I pushed the door open and stepped inside.

The same filtered sunlight that had greeted us over five years ago lit up the room, illuminating the dulled grey of the vehicle parked inside, the thick coat of dust coating the hood spiraling up at the burst of air I brought in with me.

I'd told myself I wasn't expecting anything different, and yet feeling the lukewarm glass of the windshield under my palm still made bile rise up in my throat.

Because she wasn't here, because she couldn't be afraid of me any longer, because I hated all of us for letting this happen, I spun, reeling, sending the storage bins still stacked against the wall toppling, parts spilling over, metal clattering across concrete and pinging off glass.

I wrenched the door open, making a sound somewhere between a shout and a sob at the sight of the bags still resting on the floor, the lockbox still latched and nestled beneath the driver's seat, looking for any other sign or indication that this could mean what I wanted it to, and coming up with nothing, nothing, nothing.

Dissolving her escape, her future, her freedom.

She'd never made it this far.

And so within a week, after going paperless with bills and tying up loose ends and explaining to my friends and family that no, I was not having a mental breakdown, I was off.

I drove day-to-day, going off handfuls of paper she'd written on and offhand comments she'd made throughout the years, finding old places we'd gone and places we'd wanted to. I drove west to the coast and all the way north, turned tail and started making my way back. I stopped when I wanted to. I went when I wanted to. I did what I wanted and what she wanted, and I wrote home twice a week, as I'd promised. In bad weather, I'd work on the tiny wood wrens I left along the way. It gave me something to do with my hands and my head besides thinking.

And now I'm stranded in Kansas with no plan and nobody to talk to, because in letting my need for catharsis control me, I shoved everyone else out of the way.

After a few hours of black coffee refills and aimless internet surfing, I make my way back across the street to the shop, wandering over to a nondescript silver sedan and then hovering there until the servicer sees me and comes over, wiping his hands on his jeans.

"Is this a '98?" I ask like I don't know, and I run my hand over the hood as if it's going to speak to me, though these cars are everywhere and I've jumped at every one of them.

"Yup. Still runs like new, though, 'cept for the normal wear and tear. The girl who owns it sure loves it. Reliable cars, these old things."

"Sure are," *that's why I picked it.* I thrum my fingers against the roof, turning to face him and nodding toward my car, "how's it going?"

"The part should be in tomorrow. We'll trim a few bucks off for the hassle. We've got a car you can borrow out front."

"Thanks. And don't worry about it. I'd do it myself if I could bring my garage with me."

"You work with cars?"

"My dad owns an auto shop near Sopchoppy. A little ways south of Tallahassee. I grew up in it."

He nods approvingly, folding his arms and nodding to the sedan behind me.

"It's a good way to learn, that's for sure. She says she did, too. Girl knows her way around a vehicle. She stays to watch from time to time."

Don't let anyone charge you for anything on your car without knowing why they're doing it. If you already know what's wrong, you can make sure you don't get ripped off.

Small towns are good for a few things: gossip, stunted social development due to only interacting with the same ten kids for your entire life, and staying in small towns forever. I belong somewhere like here, this tiny little postage stamp of a city, and yet a few hours standing still in one and I'm already lapsing back into the standstill that pushed me out onto the road in the first place.

"Give me a call when she's ready," I gesture toward my car as I make my way out of the garage, patting the trunk of the sedan as I go.

The loaner doesn't purr like my own, but it runs. I stop at a minuscule bookstore and go through maps and books of the town's history, and, when I find virtually nothing because it's Kansas and I've already passed the nearest major city, I ask the woman behind the desk, who tells me that after her husband died, she spent a lot of time driving around the back roads in Haven.

"It's comforting," she says, patting my hand with her paper-soft one, and that sounds like just what I'm looking for. After staying the night in the first major chain hotel I've been in on my entire trip – bleach-white showers and hospital corners on the blankets – I spend the day lazily updating my blog and my parents, even calling home to hear their excitement instead of just reading it. Around four I pick up my car and head southeast, taking only dirt roads and stopping at tiny diners to try their specials. By the time I arrive, dusk is already beginning to settle over the sleepy little town, so I take a right and find the only motel for miles. The room is outdated, and the lights are dim. I lie on top of the blankets in my sleeping bag, planning out tomorrow until my eyes close by themselves and I fall into an exhausted sleep.

68 – Sawyer

Today is all about the adventure, and so I go weaving down backroads where the leaves are starting to change, dirt billowing out behind me. I stop to ask directions from people walking their dogs or playing with their kids in their front yards. Everyone is more than happy to point me in the direction of scenic routes and short hikes to the river, their favorite spot to eat in town and their favorite place to bring visitors. Each stop yields entirely different answers than before, and since I have no plan at all I follow every one of them. An elderly couple comes out to greet me when they see me taking pictures of the sprawling tree overtaking their front yard.

"I'm sending pictures back home to my parents," I explain once I've introduced myself, "it makes them feel better to see where I've been."

"That's a good boy, listening to them," the wife, Mauve, elbows her husband, "see, Gene, he does what he's told."

"So, what brings you out here?" Gene asks, ignoring her except for a subtle wink in my direction, "this town isn't exactly what you'd call a tourist attraction."

"I heard it was a good place to find what I'm looking for."

"Where are you headed?"

"Florida. Home," and then I'm telling them the story, because they nod and smile and shake their heads in shame at all the right places. Mauve takes my hand in hers and pats it with soft but steady resolution.

"You're doing a good thing. This is a good way to grieve."

"It felt a lot like running, at first. But I think it's starting to help. She would have loved this – but in all honesty I probably wouldn't have ended up out here if she'd been with, since she never would have let my car sound so bad for so long."

Gene laughs, and something about the two of them is so genuine that I can't help but laugh, too.

"Well, you're in luck, coming out this way. Not too long ago – just a few summers ago, I think it was – they built one of those tiny houses just down the road a ways. We visit the lady there from time to time. Quiet place. I'm sure she'd love to hear your story."

They give me small-town directions – a left at the water tower, a right at the leaning shack, etc. – and Gene gives me a firm handshake and pat on the back.

"It was good to meet you, Sawyer," he says, and Mauve smiles.

"It was good to meet you, too," I say, and after a very brief hesitation, she pulls me in for a hug.

They stand on their lawn and wave as I drive away, holding hands and leaning into each other, and they look like home.

69 - Sawyer

The owner of the tiny house is nearing the upper edge of middle aged, her hair growing silver around the roots and her eyes perpetually crinkled at the edges. She shakes my hand with both of hers and sets the tiny wren I hand her on the surface of the soil in a potted plant on her front stoop.

I don't tell her about the trial, don't tell her about how Wren died or who she was or what it really feels like – most people don't actually want to know. I give her the skeleton of a story, the barest, most detached version I can muster so that she gets the idea without having to sympathize too much.

"It's always so much harder when they're young," she pats my hand comfortingly, her head tilting to one side, "that kind of heartache is so much more unexpected."

She doesn't have the look about her – the vague fog behind her eyes, the haunted shadow to her bones – she isn't speaking from experience, only from her heart. So I just nod, and thank her, and don't burden her with the whole truth.

She takes me on a tour of the house – a red tin roof and multicolored wood siding, tubes and cords running from somewhere beneath it to a complicated cluster of solar panels and then past them to a matching shed.

"I'm not really off the grid," she confesses, gesturing to her front door, "I still go grocery shopping and check my email and use a credit card. Some people around here are much more devoted to this lifestyle."

"Are there more in the area?" I ask, shielding my eyes with my hand as I gaze across her yard to where the land dips and trees dart suddenly skyward, the river burbling softly behind them.

"A little further east, there's a few. You can see them from the road for the most part, but some are a little further back. Really friendly people, even though they mostly keep to themselves."

My chest twinges a little at how much she would have loved this – an entire community stretched far and wide and yet still somehow connected.

"Thanks for showing me around," I flash my best smile, as genuine as I can fake without pushing too far, "she would have adored this place."

And she smiles back, sincere and yet still relieved that I will be gone soon, and she won't have to feel sorry for the bedraggled, sad man any longer.

"East," she repeats, waving as I duck into the loaner car, shifting and running my palms over my knees as I settle into the unfamiliar seat, "just take it slow, you'll see them."

She watches me go, as they all have, with her arms folded across her chest and her mouth twisted into a somber little smile.

70 - Sawyer

I'm about fifteen minutes outside of town when I see it, and that's just because I'm looking.

Tiny and unassuming, sharp grey roof jutting upward from the trees, the a-frame house is no more than 200 square feet. A footpath runs a few yards to another structure – this one made mostly of windows and foggy mismatched panes, the smudged green of leaves visible through the glass. A silver vehicle is parked around back, the bumper barely visible from the walkway.

Several raised gardens line the lawn, stepping stones crisscrossing between them. Potted plants frame the porch and take the place of railings up the few short stairs.

I park the car and step out, slowly, listening for any sign that someone is home aside from the dog resting underneath the front bay window.

"Hello?" I call, pausing every few feet to admire the neat rows of frost-withered but clearly well-loved flowers, feeling slightly ashamed that I can't even keep a cactus alive. Whoever lives here could probably grow daises in the desert.

"Anyone home?"

There's only near-silence, the dog opening his mouth in a hushed bark and shifting slightly.

"I heard about your house," I raise my voice a little as I come closer to the staircase and take the first step, earning another quiet snort from the dog, 'your, uh, neighbors said you might let me take a look around?"

I knock, but there's no response, so I fumble around in my bag for a pen and a wooden bird and stoop to write a note for the owner.

"Sorry, I must have had my music too loud," says a voice behind me, and as I stand I reach out to grab the corner of the little house for support.

Because there she is, barefoot and light and glowing, the sun shining bright on her skin and her hair and her face, and I realize in this moment that in all the time I had known her she had only been growing darker.

"Sawyer," Wren says, and time stands still.

71 - Wren

He's changed so much in the years that I've been gone.

His barely-too-shaggy hair has been trimmed neatly around his neck and ears, the top just long enough to be swept back from his tired eyes. His features have hardened and set into a comfortable ruggedness that still somehow hasn't smudged out his boyish charm. He's still got his ever-present shadow of blond stubble accenting his sharp jawline, his crooked mouth slightly agape at the sight before him: a ghost, a memory, a liar.

"Sawyer," I say again, and he takes one step down toward me, his legs wobbling.

And then he lurches toward me, and I'm crying and so is he, crushing me to his chest like he's trying to pull me inside of him. And I understand completely because I didn't realize until this moment just how hollow I've been.

"I hoped," he says, his voice muffled in my hair and my neck, "I hoped, but I was so afraid I was wrong."

"I never thought you'd actually find me," I'm trying to be coherent but the words are coming out jagged and tearful, "I left little clues, I hoped you would understand but it was all I could do. I'm so sorry. I'm so sorry."

"You got out," he inhales, pulling away just enough to nudge his forehead against mine, "don't say you're sorry; you got out, Wren."

Instinctively, I jolt, my eyes flashing toward the street

before they dart back to his face as though magnetized to it.

"Sawyer, maybe you should come inside."

"Okay," he says, but he doesn't move, still staring at me like if he blinks I'll vanish before his very eyes. I link my fingers through his and pull him back up the steps, pushing the front door open and letting Fidget squeeze between us, stopping only momentarily to sniff Sawyer's legs and wag his tail enthusiastically before trotting over to his water dish.

"He's a rescue. He's six," I tell him, and he nods, looking mildly shell-shocked, "I kept his name, since I didn't keep mine. I go by Ellie, here. It's short for – "

"Ellis," he finishes, but softly, like his head hasn't quite caught up yet.

I've never felt like I needed to fill the silences with Sawyer, but now I can't stop talking, leading him to the couch and sitting down next to him so that our knees are touching and I'm still holding tight to his hand. I'm babbling about things that aren't important and over six years have passed since I've seen him in real life and he's seen me at all, and he can't seem to stop staring at me. I tell him about adopting Fidget from the humane society, and about slowly putting together the house I'd always dreamed of, how between the money we'd stored in the lockbox and the significant sum our friends at the garage had compiled over the years I'd been able to build – with help, of course – the entirety of it and most of the greenhouse before I'd taken a job in town to avoid cutting too much into my savings. How easy it was, once I explained that I was running from an abuser, to give security deposits in lieu of my social security number or credit card information.

"Everyone was so understanding, Sawyer. They didn't ask any questions once I told them my ex was looking for me. I kept moving a lot, at first, and it wasn't until people had stopped looking for me and started focusing on the trial that I could finally stop running and settle here."

"So you know. What happened to him."

I finally fall silent, and he nods once, slowly.

"Life without parole. No more chances."

"Good," I say, and I mean it.

"Is that why you didn't tell me?"

And he sounds so broken, so desperate to understand why and how I could have done this without him.

"I didn't tell you because I had to go. Because if I'd come to you looking like I did that day, you'd have killed him yourself. Because once I was far enough away and I finally watched the news and saw what was happening, it was too late to go back, and I knew that if you knew I was alive you'd lie for me, and I couldn't let you put yourself at risk like that."

"And after?"

"I just had to hope. That you'd be okay or that you'd piece it together if it was even enough for you to notice. I couldn't leave much, Sawyer. I couldn't risk it. I couldn't risk you."

"I still can't believe this is real," he says, still wide-eyed and searching and stunned, "I came here because my car was breaking down and I didn't have anything to do today, and this old couple told me about the house, and – "

"And you saw my car in the shop when you stopped at a local place to get your work done instead of a chain."

Of course I read his blog, of course I follow his every word to make sure that he's doing alright, of course I have been since before the trial, before I disappeared, from the very first entry when it was just a high school project that none of us took seriously and most of us abandoned as soon as the class was over.

"You've been reading."

"Every post."

"There's no way you knew all of this would happen."

"No," I shake my head, and both of us are staring at each other like this is a dream and we're about to wake up, "no, I had no idea. It was a reach. But this was my one chance and when I went back in to get my car they said you'd left, and I thought that was it. But then Ruth told me she'd sent you out this way – "

"Ruth?"

"The owner of the bookstore," I'm breathless, trying to slow myself down so that he can understand how this has all come together, how deliberate everything had to be to avoid giving either of us away, "she's my boss. I told her that an old friend of mine from the system might come looking, but that I hadn't seen him in years and that it was a treasure hunt. She loves stuff like that. She sent you to at least three diners, didn't she?"

"You work at a bookstore?"

"We have time," I tell him, leaning in and holding his hands tightly between mine, forcing him to look upward out of his fog and see me, "Sawyer, it's okay. We have time."

72 - Wren

He'd been good, but I hadn't fallen for it. I still walked on eggshells, still bowed my head and smiled at all the right times in all the right places. He still sidestepped and backpedaled and manipulated.

After we'd fight – me cowering, him roaring – he'd come to me with gentle hands and apologies, taking my silence and compliance as forgiveness. His nervousness that he had so carefully concealed from the beginning slowly faded until he was sure that he had regained control. And that was all he really needed.

The day Sawyer remembers – the day I came to him defeated, apologizing, telling him with no uncertainty that I'd made a mistake too big to go back on – that was the day things fell into place.

I was ready to leave. I'd spent the last six months biding my time, transferring handfuls of cash to prepaid visas, writing letters to Sawyer that I hoped would explain to him why it had taken me so long to go. He was supposed to know everything ahead of time. He was supposed to be able to explain it to our parents.

But I'd made one mistake. My bag was ready and hidden in the vent near the front door – containing my car key and my new IDs and everything I'd need to get from there to somewhere far away fast.

I must have not closed it fully, some day when he came home too soon and I scrambled to shove it out of view and fit the screws back in place. Because when I reached into my bag on the first bus to pay my fare, my hands came up empty and I realized with a sickening swoop in my chest that the wallet containing everything I needed to disappear had never made it out of the house.

And it still could have been alright; I could have suffered through nothing but the suspicion that came with a slightly prolonged absence, if I'd gone back and tried again the next day.

Except that I'd left my engagement ring on my bedside table, where Cam was sure to find it.

"I messed up," I told Sawyer, but I needed those papers to be able to leave, and so I needed to go back, "I messed up," but I didn't think anything was going to end the way it did.

"Are you leaving me?" he was waiting when I walked in the door, and I was ready, having received every text message and every voicemail he'd left me in the last hour.

"Of course not," I scoffed, like the idea was ridiculous, like it hadn't been consuming my mind every waking moment for the last five years.

"What's this, then?" he held the ring up between his thumb and pointer finger, thrusting his hand toward me, "where have you been?"

"I had to stop at the bank to get cash for the work potluck. I was scared I lost it – I must have forgotten to put it back on after I put lotion on this morning – "

"Don't lie to me, Wren. Where do you think you're going to go? Who do you think is going to want you?"

I stared at him silently, trying to catch my footing, trying to calculate how I was going to get out of this without him being able to tail me, now that he was sure he knew.

"You think you can just walk away from this? After everything I've been doing for you to try and fix us for the last six months, you think you can just walk away?" he flung the ring against the sliding glass door, and it pinged off and zipped across the floor, rolling under the cupboards by the kitchen doorway.

"I'm not going anywhere, Cam. I promise."

"Pick it up, then."

I considered walking out. I considered running back to Sawyer or home or even the police, but I knew that if I did I would never make it past the front steps without him seeing it as justification for his anger.

Instead, I crossed the room and knelt to retrieve the ring, keeping my head down and my body braced for impact. He watched as I eased myself to my knees, reaching under the cupboard and running my palm along the floor, my eyes unfocused to keep him in my peripheral vision.

"Do you really think you can just leave? Has that ever worked out for you in the past? You can't leave me, Wren. I promise that if you ever pull anything like this again, I will make your life a living hell. Do I make myself clear?"

You already do, I thought, but before I could decide whether or not to say it out loud, his hand closed around my throat and he hauled me back to my feet.

"Cam," I gasped, my fingers scrabbling at his, "please."

He raised me upward until my feet were barely touching the ground, my shoulders pressed crookedly into the angle the cabinet and my toes scraping against the laminate.

"I did everything you asked of me," he hissed, leaning in so his nose brushed mine and his words ran over my skin, "and you think you're going somewhere? You think you're going *anywhere?*"

"I just forgot, I forgot, I forgot," I pleaded, my vision spotting as his grip tightened, "I wouldn't leave you; I love you, please."

He released me almost instantly, my back sliding against the wall and my hands reaching out instinctively as my legs wobbled beneath me.

"You haven't said that in so long," he said, brushing my hair back from my face, not seeming to notice that I shuddered away, recoiled at his touch, "God, Wren. It's like you forgot."

It's like I finally realized that I have no idea what love is, but it's not this.

"I thought you'd given up on us, do you get that? I couldn't stand losing you," he pressed rough kisses to the space above my ear, my neck, his hands lowering from my shoulders and moving their way down to my hips.

"Wait, Cam," I pushed him away, gently, by the wrists, my vision blurry and my throat still tight.

"No, it's okay – I love you, too."

His eyes were wild, pushing me backward onto the cupboard and pulling my face toward his forcefully.

"Cam, please wait – "

"I just needed to hear it, Wren, it's okay."

And my head was spinning and my nerves were raw and I was still reeling, though already my head was whispering my body to relax, breathe, and let this pass, too.

"Get *off* of me," I threw my hands between us, desperately, and he stumbled.

The leg of the table caught his ankle and he went down fast, his legs splaying out ungracefully in front of him and his arms barely breaking his fall. My blood ran cold and I lowered my feet back to the floor, holding my breath.

"You bitch," he snarled, lurching forward and grabbing me by my ankle as I tried to run, pulling my feet out from under me and sending me sprawling, my heart in my throat.

"I'm sorry –" I gasped, kicking wildly, catching him once in the shoulder and once in the jaw as he advanced, but he didn't slow. One knee pinned my legs to the floor, his hands closing over my throat again with crushing finality.

"Why does it always have to be like this, Wren?" he pleaded, his eyes wet, his nostrils flaring, "what happened to us?"

My mouth opened and closed uselessly, my hands pawing weakly at the air between us.

"You used to understand. What happened to you? You used to care about me – about us. What is it going to take to get you to be like that again?"

And he must have thought that I was trying to say what he wanted to hear, because he released ever so slightly, just enough for me to get the words out.

"You're going to have to kill me."

He almost looked sorry, for a second. His grip faltered and his leg slid between mine, one hand lifting as though he meant to caress my cheek.

And then my head slammed into the floor, and he dragged himself back to his feet, pacing.

"I tried to be better for you," he cried, running a hand through his hair, "I tried to be better, and you made it so *hard.*"

I glanced toward the door, toward the grate concealing my last chance out, and I wondered, fleetingly, if it was worth it.

"Where are you gonna go, huh?" he reeled, and when I took a crawling, lurching step toward the door he grabbed one of the glasses sitting on the hutch by the decanter and hurled it so that it exploded against the frame, sending fragments of glass raining down across the floor and over my skin, "do you think Sawyer's still going to want you when he finds somebody to love who isn't so screwed up? Who isn't so broken? Do you think Doug and Penny signed up for your whole life? They signed up for four years because you're a charity case," he whipped another glass, this one hitting the corner near me and spraying me with shards, "you're kidding yourself if you think you're their first choice, if you think you're anyone's first choice."

I caught a glimpse of myself in the full-length mirror beside the front door; my neck already smudging black and blue. A drop of blood dotted my cheekbone, and I reached up and gingerly brushed the diamond of glass from it, flinching slightly.

"I made you something. I gave you chances you never would have had. Do you really think you could have ended up in a house like this on your own? That you could have ended up with a good job right out of high school and a chance to be the wife of somebody worthwhile? I gave you everything, and you haven't appreciated *any of it.*"

"You didn't give me anything," I felt the tremor in my voice, watched his eyes narrow and his stance change, "you made me work for everything – you forced me to – "

"I never forced you to do anything," he crossed the space between us in a flash, kneeling to grab me by a fistful of hair, yanking me toward him, "you'd better be very careful what you accuse me of. I know all about your little getaway car, you know. How you take it for drives now and then. Parading around in it. You should know better than to think you're smarter than me."

"Let go of me."

"Let go of me," he mocked in a falsetto, "I told you I wasn't my father's son. I told you. I promised you that I'd do my best to be better and I was, wasn't I?" he nudged my jaw with his nose, lowering his voice so that it rumbled in my bones, "don't you remember how much better I was? Don't you remember how good it was?"

I remember not being so scared all the time.

"I don't want to hurt you, Wren. I try so hard to be good to you, and then you do things like this. And look at the mess we've made now. This all could have been avoided," his voice was gentle, his breath hot in my ear, "why can't you put in a little effort yourself?"

I didn't answer, holding myself stiff and unyielding to his touch, keeping my eyes downcast.

"I don't expect much from you, Wren," he tucked my hair behind my ear, kissing my temple softly, "but this goes both ways. I just need to hear that you want this. I need you to value this as much as I do."

I promise I'll be careful with you. I love you. I don't want you to feel this way, baby. Let me help you. We're so good for each other. Just tell me it's okay, and it will be.

"You said you loved me. Did you mean it?" he only seemed encouraged by my lack of response, "please don't lie to me, I can't take it."

Don't make me out to be the bad guy here, Wren. You never told me to stop. I didn't do anything you didn't want me to do.

"Don't lie to me," he was sharper now, and when he tugged on my wrist again, I tripped, and the glass crunched beneath my bare feet. I sucked air between my teeth sharply and stumbled backward, leaving bloody imprints of my toes in my wake and drawing his eye downward.

"I'm sorry," I blurted immediately, freezing in place so as to not track it any further, "I'll get it, I'm sorry."

"Let me see," and he swept me up and carried me to the table, sitting me on the edge of it and kneeling to inspect my soles, his hands feather-light and his brow furrowed, "it's nothing. You won't be going anywhere anytime soon, though, now will you?"

He raised his eyes to meet mine, his words deliberate, and pressed his thumb into a fragment, sending shooting pain up my leg.

"He's been calling you, this whole time," he mused, sliding my phone from his pocket and dangling it between two fingers when I looked toward my purse in confusion, "do you think I'm stupid? Did you tell him you were leaving? Was he your getaway? Is he waiting somewhere for you right now?"

"I already told you I wasn't leaving –" he pressed down again, and I swallowed a cry.

"Where is he?"

"I don't know, I haven't seen him all day – "

"Do you think I can't smell him on you? Do you think I don't know when you're lying to me?" he wrenched me forward so that I was barely balancing on the edge of the table, his hand climbing up my leg to my hip and pulling me to him as he stood, "where's he waiting, Wren?"

"He's not – "

"You've been pulling away from me, pushing me away this whole time," he leaned in and I leaned back, and he scoffed, his lip curling, "is he worth it, Wren? Is he worth tearing everything that we had apart? Is he still going to want you when there's no more sneaking around and he realizes that all you are is a tease?"

"It's never been like that; you know it's never been like that with him."

"Do I, Wren? Because I don't think I do. It's not someone else planning to take you away from me, is it? Where is he waiting?"

"What are you going to do to him?"

"Nothing," he smiled, that lopsided grin that I used to love before it grew so cruel, "I just think it's time that the two of us actually talked, don't you?"

I hesitated just enough before I answered, so that his brow arched and his impatience simmered under his skin.

"He's waiting at Ochlockonee. I'm supposed to meet him in half an hour." A lie, and yet he swallowed it without hesitation because it was what he wanted to hear.

He glanced at his watch, then nodded, propping his hands on either side of me.

"What was your plan?"

"I was going to meet him there. We were going to have my car towed back here so you wouldn't know where to start looking."

"Why don't you go ahead and make that call now? We wouldn't want to stray too far from the plan, would we?"

He pressed the phone into my hand, and I obeyed, doing my best to keep my voice even as I spoke to the insurance dispatcher but knowing she would remember this call, anyway.

"Please don't hurt him," I whispered as he plucked it from my grasp once again, scrolling through the missed calls from Sawyer, "please – he'll listen if you tell him I don't want to see him anymore. He'll listen to you."

"I'm not going to hurt him, Wren," he set the phone down next to me, wiping his hands on his jeans, "that was never the idea. I just want to show him that if he really cares about you at all, he'll stay away from you from now on."

He grabbed my head and jerked it downward, slamming it into his knee and letting me topple onto my side with a gasp. Blood gushed from my nose and between my teeth, and the world tilted sharply.

"We just have to make this convincing," he nudged me with his foot just hard enough to send me sprawling, waited until I'd regained my balance to do it again, "I just need something to show him, so that he knows what will happen if he tries this again."

I lurched toward the kitchen, focused, not feeling the shards dig into my skin as I crawled, letting the blood flow down my wrists and over my palms.

"Wren, the more you fight, the more this is actually going to hurt," he stooped to lift me, then slammed me down on my back in the fragments, cringing slightly when I howled in pain and clamping his fist over my mouth.

"This is enough, it's enough," I pleaded when he let go, because we both knew that it took far less than this to scare Sawyer.

"You were going to leave me, baby," he sighed, crouching over me so that I was pinned in place, smoothing my hair back before settling with his wrists on his knees, "did you think I wouldn't care about that?"

When he reached for me again – slower this time – I dragged my palms over his face, streaking his skin with my blood.

He reeled backward, eyes wide, smearing his fingers over his cheek and then holding them out in front of him in disbelief.

"Don't pretend this is about anyone but you," I said, and his eyes focused back on mine and he lunged.

73 - Wren

He shook me, violently, before he left. I let my eyes flutter open and then roll back shut, my head lolling.

"Wren?" he shook me again, then leaned in, listening for a hitch in my breathing, but I let my limbs sprawl as he released me and stood. I waited, for the sound of the shutter on my phone and then for the door to slam behind him, the growl of my engine fading as he peeled out of the driveway and down the street.

I dragged myself to my knees, then to my feet, my head ringing and my body leaden.

Slowly, deliberately, I shoved my bare feet into a pair of leather boots and laced them tight, the soles sticking and prickling with each step. I leaned into the counter as I washed the blood from my face until the water stopped running red, and then some.

This is your one chance. This is it. Go. Now.

After passing the mirror again, I wrapped a scarf around my neck and tied it close, pulling my hair forward and brushing my bangs as far over my eyes as I could. I fished the wallet from the hollow behind the grate. Pulling a sweatshirt on despite the warm air and tugging the sleeves down over my palms, I took a deep breath and I stepped out into the night.

"I walked six blocks to a bus stop, in case they looked at footage near the house later," I tell Sawyer, his face illuminated only by the flames of the wood stove, "and I still had to walk another three miles to get to the garage."

Dazed, exhausted, my head still ringing and his words still rattling between my ears, I emptied the contents of the lockbox into my purse, then slipped back out into the night and kept walking. Later, if he tried to tell anyone about the vehicle, which he had undoubtedly fitted with a tracking device just as he'd done to my own car, they would find it here, untouched. I couldn't have planned it if I'd tried.

In the morning, I paid cash for a Craigslist car that could hardly break 45 without sputtering and hissing and drove until the tank was nearly empty. By then the sun had risen and I could cover my shadowed eyes with dark glasses, though I wasn't too concerned about making myself unmemorable to someone who was willing to sell their car immediately for a handful of cash at 6am. Back in Clearwell, Cam wiped my blood from his hands and the interior of my car and called a taxi back to the house. This was his downfall – in using my vehicle to try and catch Sawyer off guard, his only alibi was the taxi driver, who picked him up from Ochlockonee while my car sat waiting for the tow truck that would eventually come for it and send everything into motion. It wasn't until months later, after I'd left the original and made my way from city to city using only busses, that I bought my current car, the same make and model as the one I'd left resting in the garage.

"I was a suspect too, at first," Sawyer tells me, and I'm relearning the planes of his face because so much has changed, "they hauled me in for questioning, took things from my house, my computer, my phone."

I know about the traces of my blood found in the crevasses of his sink drain, a small fistful valuables I kept safe in his bedside table drawer, my DNA left all over his apartment – places that Cam told them it shouldn't be – all packed up into plastic bags labeled "evidence" and filed away.

"I wouldn't have kept running," I promise him, though I know by now it might not mean much, "if it had been you, I wouldn't have stayed gone."

"Don't," he looks up, his eyes sharp, "I wouldn't have wanted you to."

"I couldn't let you go to prison for – "

"I couldn't let you stay with him. Do you think I wouldn't have taken the fall if I'd known you were safe? I would have, Wren. I wouldn't have hesitated."

"I know," I breathe, and his expression softens, firelight in his eyes, "that's why I would have come back."

He's staring at me, too, the wood crackling and the light flickering on his skin, and finally I can accept the quiet without having to fill it with explanations.

"Don't feel guilty about him being there," he says after a minute, still not dragging his eyes from mine, "you just left. Everything that happened after was his doing."

"I know," and though I've known it the whole time it still relieves me to hear it in his voice, "I just left."

Because if he hadn't had the car towed, if he hadn't wiped clean the interior, if he hadn't bleached the floors and the walls and hidden my ring, if he hadn't gone so far to conceal what he'd done, I would have just gone missing. I would have just run away, and that would have been the end of it.

But he did, and so I was dead, and my friends and family suffered, and for that he deserved prison, deserved to not know.

"I'm proud of you," he whispers, and in the dim light I can see the tears in his eyes, the slight upward tilt to the corner of his mouth, "please don't hate yourself for becoming the person you needed to be to survive."

"I missed you," I crawl over to him, run my fingers through his hair, "I wanted to call you, or write to you. To let you know that I was okay, that I'd made it, but I couldn't risk it. And then the trial was over, and you were getting thousands of hits on your website, and people were waiting outside your house. I could tell how tired you were of everything. I thought once things died down, you'd be able to move on. That things would get better for you."

"I thought you were dead," he brushes his thumb over my cheek and I realize I'm crying again, "that's not really something you get better from."

"I lied to you," I swallow hard, try not tremble too much, "if I'd let you in on more, you might have known right away. You might have been able to get past it."

"Yeah, and I'd have lied on the stand. That's called perjury, and it's illegal even if you don't get caught."

'How are you so lighthearted about this? How are you not mad at me, or crying like I am, or – "

"Mad at you? Wren, you did exactly what I wanted you to. A little sloppy from the last-minute alterations, but he tried to kill you. He'd have ended up in prison anyway," he actually laughs, short and disbelieving, "of course I'm not mad at you."

"Why aren't you crying?" I ask after a pause, and he laughs again, this time for real, gently butting his forehead against mine.

"Why are you?"

"Because I love you and it hurts," I laugh, tears streaming freely down my cheeks.

"I know," he says, closing his eyes for the first time since he got here, his head resting against mine, our noses brushing.

"I want to absorb you into my skin so that you can't leave,"

I tell him, and he laughs again, pressing his lips to the space between my eyes, "I want to inhale you and keep you in my lungs."

You don't realize how much you need physical contact until the only kind you receive is accidental – brushing against someone as you pass them on the street, your fingertips touching as you hand someone a book.

"It's okay, Sparrow," he says, while I hide my face in the curve of his neck and breathe in deep, "we've got time."

74 - Wren

To avoid drawing suspicion from the guys, I started out taking only handfuls of cash from the can at a time. Crumpled bills shoved into my pocket and exchanged for prepaid credit cards each time I went grocery shopping. Separate transactions, for when Cam combed the receipts for anything he deemed suspicious.

I stashed them behind the grate in the living room, until I could bring them to the lockbox in the car. I watched my funds grow and felt hope begin to grow hesitantly in the base of my throat. For every loose end tied off, for every stepping stone set in place, I started to believe that I had a future.

I also found myself looking for reasons to stay.

At this point I understood; he was abusive, he was manipulative, that no amount of control would ever be enough. I knew I had to get out.

But it wasn't that I'd be staying for him.

If I left, I had to commit. I had to go no-strings-attached, no faltering. If I left, I would be leaving the only family I'd ever had behind, because including them in my absence would be implicating them in it. If I left, it would be ages before I could see them again.

Sawyer so desperately wanted to help, and he was willing to do whatever it took. But I was serious when I said that I couldn't take him with me, and risk him losing the sunshine inside him. He had a home and a life and a family that was permanent and real, and while I knew I deserved better than what Cam was giving me, I couldn't align myself with the idea that I deserved someone as good as Sawyer. To wrench him away from all of that meant risking him; and regardless, anyone who knew where to find me would be in danger, at least for awhile.

If I didn't come back, he would find ways to draw me in. Another fire, an accident, something on a scale so grand that I'd be made aware of it no matter how far I ran – and he knew I'd be looking for it, too.

Leaving should have seemed like the easiest thing in the world, the simplest, the only option. But now that it was looming closer, the parts of my brain that had been rewired to handle the life I was living were backpedaling furiously. Leaving would be effortless, once I pushed past the adrenaline and the fear of being caught. Staying gone in spite of everything I knew him to be capable of was an entirely different story.

But then I would catch myself hyperventilating at the smell of bleach in the detergent aisle while shopping, or reeling backward when my boss reached over my head to grab a mug from the cupboard at work, or scrambling to clean up a mess someone else had made, and my resolve strengthened.

If I wanted to be strong enough to get out, I had to believe that everyone else would be strong enough to live with the repercussions. I had to stop taking responsibility for the things that he did.

75 - Sawyer

"I want to shrink down and live in your shirt pocket," she says into my throat, "I want to keep you in mine."

I'm not crying because I don't think I can – everything I've been holding off for the last ten years is swelling up in the back of my throat and lungs and my heart feels like it's about to give out completely, and everything she's saying makes sense to me even though it means nothing at all.

"Are you hungry?" she says suddenly, pulling backward and letting cool air take her place, and I want to pull her back and keep her wrapped around me, afraid that if she gets too far away she'll vanish again, "we haven't eaten in hours, I can make dinner, I – "

I don't say anything, and she must see something in my face because she settles back onto her heels and stares at me, smiling faintly, the light from the fire dancing on her skin, casting shadows in the hollows of her collarbones and her wrists. Her eyes are bright and her shoulders are relaxed, her features soft and content. Never have I seen her look so bright, and it doesn't elude me that my presence in her life was included in that darkness.

"You look gorgeous," I revel in the sound of her laughter, the flush that's clearly visible even in the faint light, "I don't think I ever realized your full potential, Sparrow."

"Yeah, you don't look so bad yourself," her laughter fades but her smile stays, and with anyone else the silence would be unbearable, the way she seems to be taking inventory of every inch of me would feel like scrutiny, "look at us, Sawyer. Look how much we've grown."

She extends her hand and I raise my palm to meet hers, curling the tips of my fingers over hers so she grins again at the slightness of her hands in comparison to mine, just as she always has.

"I feel like I have so much to tell you, but I really don't think I do," she says, gently tracing the lines on my palm with her fingertips, "there are things to show you, maybe – but that can wait until morning. I've worked really hard on all of this. I haven't had anyone to show it to."

"There's time," I say again, because for the first time in years there is and if I don't say it then it doesn't feel real, "we've got all the time in the world."

Her smile falters only slightly, and I hate myself for making it quaver.

"Don't worry," I tell her, reaching out to cup her chin, and she turns her face into my hand and presses her lips to it, her eyes shadowed, "we don't have to think about anything yet."

"I used to watch people," she says, her eyes closed, lashes dark on her cheeks, "I'd see people older than me by ten, twenty, thirty years, and I'd feel my heart clench, something like longing for the chance to be them. To be anyone but who I was or where I was. And now I have it – I have that chance, and that time, and I don't know what to do with it because I lost everything else."

"You didn't," I tug her back toward me, and she unfolds her legs and half-crawls half-slides her way onto my lap, her fingers tangled in the front of my shirt, her face buried in my chest, "you just got something new."

She leans backward, pulling me down, so that I'm propped up on one elbow alongside her, her hands finding mine and clasping one between hers almost absentmindedly.

"How are your parents?" she asks, softly, and I almost laugh because she's always been this way and yet it still floors me every time, "how are mine?"

"They're healing," I tell her, using the hand she's holding to brush her hair back from her face, the firelight brightening the scar on her forehead, the slight crookedness of her nose, "they're still going."

"Like you were, or better?"

"Better."

"Good," and she closes her eyes and seems to breathe it in, growing a little lighter, "you're helping?"

"I wasn't much use," I confess, and she opens her eyes, looking calm but mildly accusatory, "I'll be better, now."

"You'd better be, Sawyer Moore," my name rolls off her tongue like a spell, and her lips twist into what's almost a smirk, "I'm counting on you."

"As always," I scoff, and she laughs again, turning her face so it rests against my arm.

"You smile when I do," she muses, pressing her thumb against my cheek, "even when you try not to. Your dimples give you away."

"I missed your laugh."

"You missed everything about me, don't lie."

"That too," I inhale the vanilla-lemon scent of her, the smell of her lotion and her shampoo and her skin.

"I missed you too," she says.

76 - Wren

I wake up to the fire dying and the sunlight streaking orange across the uneven wood floors. It's cold under my bare feet as I shuffle down the short ladder to the coffee pot, pressing start and stepping over Fidget's sleeping form. His tail thumps feebly as I pass by, perching on the arm of the couch at Sawyer's feet to watch him stir.

His eyes are bleary when he first opens them, but as soon as I come into focus he smiles like my face is the best thing he's ever seen, and I pull my sweater tighter around myself and slide down so I'm sitting over his legs, facing him.

"Good morning," I say, and he exhales slowly and stretches, a shudder running through him and then me as his back arches and his knuckles crackle against each other.

"Morning."

"How'd you sleep?"

He opens one eye and one corner of his mouth tweaks, then he closes them again and grabs my wrist, pulling me down next to him and wrapping his arms around me tightly.

"Good. You?"

I don't say anything, just stare at him until he opens his eyes again and then press my icicle of a nose into the hollow of his throat, eliciting a groan of complaint and a weak attempt to wriggle away.

"Coffee's brewing. Want breakfast? I have bacon. And stuff to make waffles. I can eat all the waffles I want now. So can you."

"Wren."

"I've had words building up inside of me for six years, Sawyer. They've gotta come out sometime."

He releases me and lets me roll to my feet, jamming them into the slippers I've left by the woodstove and sliding my way back to the kitchen. I'm mixing when he sidles up behind me and reaches over me into the fridge, pulling out the bacon and turning on the stove.

"Brings back memories," I muse, whisking and plugging in the waffle iron.

"I remember a lot more cookies than waffles," he replies, inhaling deeply as the bacon starts to sizzle, "well. More cookie dough than actual cookies."

"I remember a lot more flinging of ingredients on your end," I say, flicking a puff of flour at him and watching it dance in the sunlight coming through the window, "you got more on me than in the bowls."

"What can I say; I'm not a gifted baker."

"We can't all be perfect."

He grabs me suddenly, crushing me to his chest, and I don't jump and I don't flinch and I don't pull away instinctively, because I have also spent the last six years learning how to be okay again.

"I missed you," I say, for what is probably the thirtieth time in the last twelve hours, and he nods into my hair, stamping a firm kiss to the top of my head.

"I missed you too, Sparrow."

"I never even asked you about the letters," I shimmy backward, looking up at him, "if you got them – if you read all of them. I mean, I assume you did, because you're here, and you haven't asked, so you must know – "

"I know that he deserves to rot in prison for the rest of his life while you spend the rest of yours being better than he ever imagined you could be."

"You thought that before I even left."

"That's true, I did."

"I said some stuff, in them, that you probably didn't want to hear – "

"I asked. I asked you to tell me the truth. I asked you to tell me a story, and you did. You told me everything. Don't apologize anymore, okay? Not to me. Not to anyone. You did what you had to do. You did it, Wren. By yourself. You made all of this yourself."

"I did, didn't I?"

"And I fully expect a tour as soon as breakfast is done. That greenhouse is pretty impressive."

"I have a story for every window. I promise I'll make it worth your while."

We eat in silence, sitting on the floor in front of the fire and staring at each other unblinking and trying our best not to smile. Every moment in each other's presence feels like a weight lifted, and I swear I'm so light I'm about to lift right off the ground. These unfinished wood floors, the raw walls, the mismatched windows and tin roof, all of it came from inside of me and now somebody who can see that can finally see *it*, and appreciate it in a way that only I've been able to until now.

I have worked for this and I deserve it and I am better than I've ever been.

77 - Sawyer

She walks like she weighs no more than the air, her bare toes seeming to hover above the ground as she drifts, stooping to pluck dying weeds from the gardens along the way or to point out a particular flower.

"This part took the longest. I was living in my car while I was getting all of it started. Once things started really growing, it got a lot easier, and now it does most of the work on its own."

She unlatches and pulls open the door to the greenhouse, and we're greeted by a swoop of humid air and the faint sound of trickling water. Leafy green plants lean into the aisles and arch over our heads, winding up trellises and hanging heavily with the weight of themselves.

"It has a separate generator in case something goes wrong, but I haven't had to use it at all."

She catches me staring at her and presses her lips together in a failed attempt not to smile, a slight flush spreading over her cheeks.

"What?"

"Nothing. Just… look at what you've done."

"I know," she says, and she grins like she means it, "I did this. Me."

She gives me a tour of the yard, tugging on my hand when I drift too slowly for her, eagerly showing me her tricks and tips and how she has managed to stay invisible for so long.

"It's mostly just because nobody was looking for me," she

says, and her smile is only a little sad, "if they were, I'm sure I couldn't stay gone for too long."

"I would have been," I assure her, "but things didn't go quite how we wanted them to."

"I would have told you," she reaches out, her fingers glancing briefly off my shoulder before she pulls her hand back, clenching it into a weak fist, "if there had been any good way, I would have told you. But I know – and you must know they're still watching you. Innocent or not."

And I can see in her eyes that she regrets it – that lack of presumed innocence that I'm going to have to carry with me for the rest of my life, the guilt that others have already given me based on their own conclusions – out of everything we've done, that's what she would take back.

"Well. I guess I'm not exactly innocent anymore, am I?" I brush her hair behind her ear, and she leans into my hand, eyes closed.

"You gonna rat me out, pal?" she smirks at me a second later, and I cuff her lightly without thinking, but she smiles unflinchingly.

"Of course not. I've got my own skin to save, now."

She reaches up and curls her fingers around mine, the wind lifting her hair and sending it spiraling over her shoulders.

"I was going to send you a letter. But I was scared. Scared someone else would see it, scared you'd never respond, scared you'd be mad. I left you there to pick up everything I broke and – "

She's always had a way of speaking like the words are spilling straight out of her without having time for her tongue to taste them; like they're too quick for her to feel the weight of until they're in the air and she can see them for herself.

"I missed you *so much,*" I tell her, and she trails off and slips her arms around my waist between my t-shirt and my flannel, clasping the fabric in her fists.

I wonder if she got so good at making things happen because nobody ever did it for her, or because everybody did. Somewhere along the way, the fear of becoming exactly what everyone expected made her leave herself entirely, and yet here we are; two entirely different people filling the exact same space.

78 – Wren

No amount of time will be enough, especially if it keeps moving at the rate it does.

As always, the hands on the clock seem to be spinning wildly, losing track of the hours and of daylight whenever we're together.

The important things have been said. My letters and the last two and a half days have made sure of that. Everything has changed and yet, somehow, nothing has.

"You're lighter," he says, his thumb tracing circles on my wrist as we sit cross-legged in the afternoon light, "it's like you finally realized all the potential everyone else always saw in you."

"Not everyone," I can't help the self-deprecation, even if I don't quite mean it anymore, "and really, I'm simply living the nonexistence I always was on the edge of anyway."

He rolls his eyes, but only partway, grinning and giving me a gentle rap on the knuckles with his own.

"Do you think," I say hesitantly, staring at our interwoven fingers, "do you think that it could ever be safe to tell our parents?"

When I lift my gaze, he isn't looking at me, and I falter.

"Or just hint. Something. Do you think there's any way to give them even a little bit of relief? Without putting them at risk?"

The silence drags on, but I can see the gears turning, see the sparks behind his eyes.

"I think I can come up with something," he says finally, the words hesitant but determined, "enough to answer some questions without raising any new ones."

"I can't come back. And they can't come here."

"No."

It's not a question, or a prompt. We both know that the decisions I've made to get here aren't the kind that can be undone cleanly.

They wouldn't tell. Knowing what they know since the trial – even just that, and not the grittier parts that never came out – that's still a given. But Doug and Penny have their own kids they'd have to either lie to or rope in. They'd want to see me. And then they would be implicated, too.

How could it be the right decision when it hurt so many innocent people in the process? Do the ends justify the means? I'm alive, I'm safe – but nobody knows it but me.

"Stop doing that," he says suddenly, "stop doubting. Have you been doubting yourself all this time?"

Have I? No. Not anymore.

The first days – sleeping curled in the trunk of the car so I wouldn't be visible through the windows, after the first seedy motel left me feeling less safe than anywhere else – those days were the hardest. Always moving, always checking over my shoulder, crumbling each moment that I felt safe enough to spare a moment to do so.

Each border that I crossed, each new city I disappeared into was a mixture of sharp relief and a sucking terror in the pit of my chest. The further I went, the tighter the tether pulled, until each mile left me waiting for the snap.

But it didn't come. There was no instantaneous release, no moment where the band around my lungs loosened.

There was always – still is always – the tug back to Clearwell, to the front steps of the first places that were ever really home. It's less like a bungee cord these days, more like a compass in the base of my heart always pointing me toward it. To see the relief on their faces when they realized that the nightmare I put them through was over. To feel their arms around me, to feel safe.

I stopped on the side of the road when I hadn't seen another vehicle for miles, and I screamed the kind of soul-wrenching, stomach-churning screams that you never think can come out of yourself until they do. I banged on the steering wheel, knotted my hands in my hair, let the tears and snot catch on my upper lip and drip into my lap. And then a few cities later I did it again, and again, until eventually I was too exhausted or relieved or just empty to need to anymore.

That's not to say I haven't done it since, or that there aren't still days where the pull I so strong that can barely go through the motions, instead spending hours on his blog or scrolling through the social media profiles of everyone even several degrees removed from the circles I used to frequent or flipping through the few physical pictures I've printed off since I had to leave all the others behind.

"Have you been in my room, since?"

Somehow he seems to have followed my train of thought, because he only hesitates briefly.

"I helped Penny clean it out last year."

It's good news – at least it should be – it implies closure and moving on and healing. But it still sits like a brick in the pit of my stomach.

"They gave me your books. And all the pictures of us. They got your... belongings, eventually. After things wrapped up. But it took awhile before they could..."

"Bear to look through it?"

"Yeah."

There's a pause, and then he leans over and hooks the strap of his laptop bag, rifling around for his wallet. From within it he unearths a weathered photograph and a faded and slightly dingy cord bracelet.

"You took it off?" I say, in mock indignation, at the same time he says "it broke!" rather defensively.

His eyes fall to the more faded, far dingier bracelet still tied around my ankle, and he hands me the picture.

It's an instant photo, one of those mini ones that fits into a card slot in his wallet but which has clearly been handled so frequently that it's a miracle it hasn't started separating from the backing. It's probably the last picture ever taken of me when I was Wren – the two of us sitting in the shop garage with my head tipped against his shoulder, both visibly tired from a (good) long day and bathed in golden afternoon light.

"It's something physical," he says when I hand it back to him, sliding it back into the safety of his wallet, "something that I could touch. And also something that I wouldn't have to worry about showing up on a true crime blog, since nobody else knew it existed."

He looks so heartbroken, for a single moment, as his eyes lift to meet mine again.

"Sawyer," I say, reaching out to cup his face in my hands, and he leans into my palm. There's a beat of silence, the familiarity settling over us like a blanket, "you are eating me out of house and home."

He laughs, his eyes crinkling in the corners, and just like that the light is back.

"I do have thread, by the way," I stretch to reach under the couch, sliding out the bin of miscellaneous craft supplies, "so we can remedy this situation."

By the time the sun has set, we have matching anklets hidden under our socks, and plans for a future, even if it's just tomorrow.

79 - Wren

I'm waiting on the front steps when he turns the corner, the familiar purr of his engine long alerting me of his arrival. Gravel crackles under his tires as he loops past me and around back, and I drift to my feet, pulling my sweater tighter around me as I pad barefoot around the corner.

"What is it?" he asks, right away, letting the bags of groceries fall back into the trunk, because even though his face has changed he can still read mine.

"Somebody posted a picture of you in town," I watch as the news parts his lips and bows his head, "you can't stay, Sawyer."

"Nobody saw me come this way," he says, but we both know it's futile.

"I'm committing all kinds of fraud. You're an accomplice now, yeah? Perjury, obstruction of justice?"

"Don't worry about me," he shakes his head, like the idea of him being arrested is funny, "I'm not the one we need to be concerned about."

Maybe it's an overreaction; I only know about the photo because I have alerts set up for his name on my phone. He's not really famous (or infamous) – not anymore – but there's still something deeply unnerving about someone nearby being able to identify him by sight. I'm already calculating how long the groceries will last, how long I can wait without needing to go into town.

There's a pause, a heaviness to the air.

"You can't stay," I say again, softly.

"I know."

I sit on the edge of the chair beside him while he neatly folds his clothes and arranges them in his bag, tugging the corners sharp and smoothing the wrinkles flat, dragging the time out between us. My thumbnail finds its way between my teeth and he tugs my hand back down into his, rubbing his fingertips across my palm.

"I should have just run out myself. I shouldn't have let you go anywhere."

"It couldn't last," he says, shaking his head softly, "we had a few more days than we could have expected. Best laid plans and all that."

Hardly any more words pass between us as he throws his bag over his shoulder and we trail out to his car, Fidget pacing between us and running laps around the house. We stand facing each other over the hood like we're challenging time to run out, like at any moment we'll hear the damning echo of sirens in the distance.

"How'd you know?" I ask, reaching out to grab his wrist when he finally makes a move for his door, and he stops, "how'd you know you could find me?'

"Because, Sparrow," he flashes one dimple, one sharp edge of a smirk, "murdered girls don't write suicide notes."

80 - Sawyer

She stands on her front steps, arms wrapped around herself, lifting one hand to wave as I leave her in a slow roll of dust. She looks, still, different than she ever has in my memory; her stance and her features and her presence are lighter with each moment that passes.

I still have so many questions to ask her – how many names she's had, how many people have known her and where, if she'll still be here if I come back – should I come back?

One tanned leg stutters forward, then another, and I match speed with my brake lights. We both falter, eyes locking in my rearview mirror, and then she takes one step back and I slide my foot back over to the right and she's gone, though I swear I can still see her out of the corner of my eye for miles.

She's still just as good at storytelling as she's ever been, so I can see her screaming as she crosses the state line for the first time, her illegal clunker sputtering as her heart swells in her chest. I'm standing guard in the doorway while she strips the color from her hair and snips away inches in the motel bathroom, adding the fallen locks to a trash bag with the clothes she left home in. I'm watching alongside her as she follows the story on the news from a new city every night, practicing her makeup skills in a dollar-store mirror and trying not to recognize herself at first glance. I'm watching the case develop, and go to trial, and realizing that so much went on behind the scenes that she wasn't able to see, because though it was all about her, she wasn't alive to see it.

"I still wake up sometimes sure that he's found me," she confessed in the firelight, "or that I'm still there and this is all just some coma dream."

She may be one of the only people to find comfort in the fact that eventually, only the people who loved her most will remember her. For everyone else, she will be a flicker on a television screen, a poorly lit photograph on the cover of a tabloid, a box of files in a cold storage room. Two years since her letters arrived, five since her death; with each passing year, she will wake up less afraid, because she'll wake up less memorable.

I know that she won't feel as much satisfaction as I do, knowing that he is going to spend the rest of his life sitting in a cell, guilty of everything but the crime that got him there.

81 - Wren

I am lighter than I've been in years.

There is still guilt. I'm sure there always will be. In retrospect, there are a hundred different ways in which I could have reached this result. But hindsight is 20/20, and often useless.

And it was easier at first, and stronger. I wondered if I would reveal myself in a dramatic act of self-sacrifice upon a guilty verdict – if I would once again put his well-being before my own as I had grown so accustomed to doing. I wondered if, in spite of everything, I was still weak enough to prevent him from being punished for a crime he had only attempted to commit.

It surprised me that I wasn't.

As for Sawyer: he was never surprised.

I know he'll have the words now to ease their tired minds without ever making them question it. He's always been good at that. Hopefully someday, hopefully soon, they can do for another misguided child what they did for me – this time with better results, because they've always had it in them even if I didn't have it in me.

Every important event in my life has been the result of a fluke. From start to end, I scrape on by the skin of my teeth, astonishing from time to time even myself with the resilience. I am alive. That still counts for something. I carry on. It's what I've always done.

And so, alone again, I fall back into my new routine. I check on the greenhouse. I feed Fidget. I draw the blinds as the sun sinks lower in the sky.

He's left a t-shirt, folded up and nestled into my drawer so that the familiar smell of him clings to the surrounding fabric. Tucked into the sleeve is a slip of paper with his new contact information printed neatly in crisp blue ink. He didn't ask for mine. He knows where to find me – and, as always, he's allowing me to make the decision.

I wear it to bed, knowing it will smell like me sooner this way but also knowing I will not wake up afraid tonight, wondering if everything up until now was just a dream.

As always, it is the simplest things that get me the most, and somehow just knowing that he is laughing to himself in disbelief as he continues on his adventures makes all the difference in the world.

82

Dear Sawyer Moore,

I've been thinking a lot about you, and how things have changed for you in the last thirteen years.

Thirteen years ago, you met a girl.

You traveled and you explored and you grew. Together, you made people's hearts ache with the rightness of you. Together, you deconstructed and rebuilt yourselves into something else entirely.

Together, you were the closest thing to perfection either of you had ever seen.

But things didn't stay so great, did they, Sawyer?

You watched as she unfurled and glowed and fitted herself into your life like it had been built for her all along. But you also watched her crumble, under the weight of everything she didn't know and couldn't fix.

You did everything you could, but it was never enough. You spent late nights nursing wounds and pacing in your bedroom, mind racing, trying to find a perfect solution where there was none.

And she wasn't what she had been, back when you were in this together. The light died in her eyes and even you weren't enough to reignite it. For that, she blamed herself.

She made a plan, and though she never told you, she only included you in half of it. Everything beyond that, she had to do alone. To spare you. To save you. To leave you.

Your story was a love story and a tragedy, a masterpiece of

unrivaled proportions. There was absolutely nothing about what you made each other that could have been greater than what it was.

You wrote her into your life, and in turn, the two of you wrote the world.

It's alright, Sawyer. With you, it has always been alright.

Travel far and wide and carry that with you. Go all of the places that you had planned to go, take all of the time and silence that you need. Do it for yourself, not for her, just as you would expect her to do if the situation were reversed.

Because your story is not done, and neither is hers. Keep writing it.

And when you're done, and you're ready to tell it, you know where to find me. You've always known where to find me.

Love,
Sparrow

Resources

Note: The information below is current as of the date of publication.

The National Domestic Violence Hotline is available 24/7 at 1-800-799-SAFE (7233). More information is available at **https://www.thehotline.org/**

The National Dating Abuse hotline has both call and text options available at 1-866-331-9474, as well as live chat available at **https://www.loveisrespect.org/**

The National Center on Domestic Violence, Trauma, and Mental Health offers resources at **http://www.nationalcenterdvtraumamh.org/**

The National Suicide Prevention Lifeline can be reached at any time at 1-800-273-8255. More information and resources are available at **https://suicidepreventionlifeline.org/**

Additional resources and links are available at **https://ncadv.org/resources**

Made in the USA
Monee, IL
06 June 2021